Other published works by Daniel Logan

Novels

The Spirit Gate (2014)

The Lost Portal (2011)

The First Migration (2005)

Short Stories

Climb to the Stars (2013)

Forest (2012)

Eternal Journey (2011)

Children's Stories (2008)

Across the Divide (2007)

Memoirs

The Time Capsule (2015)

Eastbound—A Route 66 Memory (2012)

THE PHOBOS EXPEDITION

THE PHOBOS EXPEDITION

*A NASA expedition to the tiny Martian
moon, Phobos, to determine if it is
extraterrestrial*

BY

DANIEL LOGAN

**A Publication of EnergyNet
Porter, TX**

The Phobos Expedition by Daniel Logan

A publication of EnergyNet, Porter, TX

Photographs used with permission in cover design:
At Home on the Range—Texas Panhandle © Gary "Dr. C." Cash
Couple on Horse Silhouette © adrenalinapura / Fotolia

*Author photograph taken in the cockpit of the Spruce Goose on display
at the Evergreen Aviation & Space Museum in McMinnville, OR*

Address comments and inquiries to:
EnergyNet
Email: Tfmauthor@aol.com

ISBN 978-1-62967-092-8

Library of Congress Control Number: 2017901507

Printed in the United States of America

First Edition: 2017

To Connie,

We are traveling life's journey together. This time to Phobos!
All my love, always

—143 d

Acknowledgments

I am thankful for the support and encouragement for my writing that I receive from my wife, Connie. When we relocated to Houston a few years ago, we downsized to a patio home only large enough for the two of us.

But for the past year, Connie has had to live with all the characters in this book—plus a few left over from my previous publications. At times our new home got a little crowded, but she put up with all of the additional guests without complaining!

My writing has given me opportunities to meet fascinating people. I became acquainted with Frank Hughes, NASA, while we both were presenting workshops at the Academy for Lifelong Learning, sponsored by the Lone Star College in Kingwood.

Frank began work at the Kennedy Space Center in 1966—the day the Apollo capsule arrived. During his career, he became responsible for all aspects of astronaut training for NASA's human spaceflight program including Space Station and Space Shuttle, training materials, simulators, and facilities. His wealth of knowledge of NASA personnel, programs, and equipment is inexhaustible and his lectures are awesome.

I am grateful that Frank provided suggestions for my manuscript and am honored that he wrote the foreword to my novel.

I appreciate those who read the preliminary draft of my manuscript and provided objective comments, Vickie Bourque, Steve Cady, and Rhea Parshall. Thanks also for the editing performed by Suzanne Bailer Smith, a writing associate, editor, and fellow author.

And to you, the reader, I want to express my thanks for choosing to read this novel. As always, I enjoy hearing from you. If you wish, contact me by email: tfmauthor@aol.com

Foreword

New science fiction always presents a vision of what is ahead in the future—whether around the corner or in some other world far away in time or space. The challenge that the author faces is to create a new set of visions that are believable based on what we know today. Yet, our knowledge or beliefs must be modified or played with into something entirely different. We have to receive a new vision in the story.

The approach that Dan Logan used in creating *The Phobos Expedition* took some new directions that have not been explored to date. He combines robotic assisted planetary exploration with sentient automatons who are envious of the humans and their emotions. They are developing a taste for human interactions. They are looking forward to taking part.

This is a big departure from Robby the Robot, a seven-foot-tall robot in the movie, *Forbidden Planet*. Dan's robots are also different from those of Asimov, who created smart and sometimes scary ones, but they did not have much of the human emotive complications that we find in *The Phobos Expedition*. We face a world like this where the robots look just like us. They think like us. And perhaps, they may also feel like we do....!

Many of us at NASA have discussed the possibilities that our robots may have intelligence exceeding our abilities added to human-like emotions. What will life be like then? What will the reaction to ordinary people be when that happens? Do we begin to develop the "Frankenstein" complex that Asimov warned us about? How will we interact with those smart beings that we are going to create? How will we react?

Dan takes us into a future where deep space travel is real and international competition is alive and well. He pushes the limits of what we know and what we hope to find. Dan encourages us to follow along and keeps us on edge with twists and turns that keep his story alive and entertaining.

The Phobos Expedition compels us to see where the journey leads.

Frank Hughes
Chief, NASA Space Flight Training (Ret.)

A Note from the Author
Phobos and Deimos

The ancient Greeks gave the fourth planet from the sun the name "Ares" after their god of war, most likely due to the planet's blood-like appearance. The Roman civilization renamed all the planets—except Earth—with Roman names, calling the red planet "Mars" for their own god of war.

The planet's two tiny moons were discovered in 1877 by Asaph Hall, the professor of Astronomy at the U.S. Naval Observatory. He named them Phobos (fear) and Deimos (terror). In Roman mythology, Phobos and Deimos were the two horses that pulled the chariot of Mars into war.

Most astronomers believe the two moons are captured asteroids. Phobos is the larger of the two with a diameter of fourteen miles. Deimos is only eight miles in diameter. Phobos is close to the Martian surface, a mere 3,700 miles above it. Phobos orbits faster than Mars rotates, completing a circuit in only seven hours. Deimos by contrast is 10,000 miles above the surface and orbits slower than Mars.

An observer on the surface of Mars would see Phobos, because of its closeness, as about one-third the diameter of our Moon. Due to its distance and tiny size, Deimos would look like a bright star. The difference in orbital speeds makes the two satellites appear to be traveling in opposite directions in the sky, Phobos rising in the West and Deimos in the East.

An April Fool's Day joke in a 1959 Midwestern paper reported that a prominent astronomer had determined both moons to be artificial satellites, beginning an urban legend that continues to resurface periodically. Various experts, including a special advisor to President Eisenhower, a Soviet astrophysicist, a NASA scientist, and even a U.S. astronaut, have suggested—some say in jest—that Phobos is an artificial satellite of extraterrestrial origin.

But no doubt, there are even stranger discoveries to be made . . . some totally new phenomenon perhaps . . . Somewhere, something incredible is waiting to be known.

—Carl Sagan, with an addendum by
Newsweek reporter Sharon Begley

Chapter One – Houston

The white stiletto, dart-like profile of the NASA Gulfstream jet stood in stark contrast to the backdrop of the severe cobalt blue sky above Houston as the plane began its descent to Ellington Field. Nearing the tops of towering cumulus clouds, the pilot spoke over the intercom to the only passenger, "Fasten your seatbelt, Ms. Lambert, we're about to encounter some turbulence. Shouldn't be too bad. We'll have you at the gate in no time."

Moira K. Lambert, Senior Director of the Science Division of NASA, closed her laptop and stowed it under her seat. Before clicking her seatbelt, she tugged at the hemline of her skirt, one a little shorter than she would normally wear for business. With a compact mirror she checked her lipstick and hair. En route to the Johnson Space Center in Houston, Moira planned to observe a live simulation of a critical, slingshot maneuver of the Ares I spacecraft. A crew was scheduled to depart the International Space Station in the vehicle the following year for an expedition to the tiny Martian moon, Phobos. Moira also looked forward to the opportunity to spend the weekend with her husband, Crawford. The two of them—he managing their ranch in Amarillo and she heading up one of the four NASA Divisions in D.C.—had few occasions to be with each other. When together though, Crawford treated her like a newlywed and outdid himself planning new ways to shower attention on her. "Even though we're about to celebrate our twenty-fifth anniversary," he always said, "because of our conflicting schedules, if you add up the total time we've spent together, we're still newlyweds."

Moira smiled at the thought of seeing him again and wondered what he had planned for the evening. Of course, Crawford was the reason for her short skirt—and her signature red, high heels. Though Moira was in her mid-fifties, she still had the legs and figure of a much younger woman. Moira dressed conservatively while in her NASA environs—not to the point of suppressing her femininity—but her forays with Crawford allowed her to emphasize her attractiveness.

The pilot slowed the jet before it penetrated the first of the clouds, but the initial jolt of turbulence reminded Moira of the oppressive, humid air mass they were entering. Subsequent encounters with the white, puffy clouds caused repeated bumps accompanied by strobe-like flashes of white alternating with blue sky outside the cabin windows. A few moments later, after a choppy descent, the plane broke into the clear beneath the cloud layer and offered a brief view of the Houston skyline—the glass-enclosed skyscrapers were reminiscent of Oz's Emerald City—before chirping to a landing. The sudden deceleration from the engine's reverse thrust pressed Moira against her belt. After applying heavy braking to allow for a turn off the runway, the pilot taxied the plane toward the hangar that housed NASA's jets.

Moira couldn't wait to be with Crawford again. The two were still very much in love, and she peered out the window across the aisle, hoping to catch sight of him, but she did not. The pilot pulled the plane onto the apron and shut down the engines. The co-pilot, dressed in a crisp uniform—white shirt and black tie complete with a brimmed cap—opened the cockpit door and stepped into the cabin. He unlatched the aircraft door and lowered the steps. "Hope you enjoyed your flight, Ms. Lambert," he said, beckoning her to deplane. "I'll get your luggage."

Moira stepped through the door and the blast of hot, damp air hit her like an ocean breaker. The deafening noise level outside forced her to cover her ears with her hands, and the wind, reeking of jet fuel, blew her hair into her face. She descended the stairs with care and fell into the arms of her good-looking Texan, Crawford, waiting at the bottom. In his Stetson and boots, he hugged her, placed a strong arm around her shoulders, and led her to the waiting limousine.

Once inside the car, the comfort of the quiet, plush, air-conditioned interior provided them the privacy to greet each other with a prolonged kiss.

"Damn, it's been too long. I've missed you," Crawford said.

"No more than me," Moira replied. "I'm not due for my business meeting until noon tomorrow. What have you got planned?"

"Dinner. Then all night—how's that sound?"

"All night what?"

"All night!"

"Absolutely perfect!"

In a small room inside a sterile lab within the Johnson Space Center Simulation Facility, Mission Specialist Taylor Carson helped Astronaut Andrew onto the exam table for his pre-flight checkup.

"You feeling okay this morning, Andy?"

"I'm fine."

"Well, we'll just run a few tests to be sure," Taylor said. "Shirt off, please."

Andy pulled his navy-blue, polo shirt with the Ares I mission logo over his head and folded it into a neat bundle before setting it on the exam table beside him. He took pride in perfection, an attribute of top priority for astronauts.

"You won't find anything out of order," he said. "I'd tell you if there were."

"No doubt, but we'll do this just for the record."

Andy had a human-like skin over his face and frame, shaded to a rich olive, a mixture of all racial tones. His voice had the qualities of a news anchor except for a tinge of a Southern accent. He could smile, frown, wink and blink, and a casual observer might not recognize him to be an android. But inside his frame, hidden from view, lay a mechanical marvel of linkages activated by a computer that could sense weight, resistance, touch, and even pain. Internal, super-powerful batteries provided the energy for the myriad of servos, solenoids, and motors required for Andy to function when he was not attached to a power supply line.

Taylor unsnapped the small cap over Andrew's belly button and inserted the twenty-seven point plug of the data-link, umbilical cord. He connected the other end to a USB port on his tablet.

"I'll have to turn you off for a few minutes," Taylor said. "I don't want you to feel the discomfort from the computer probing all your systems."

Andy's expression turned to one of chagrin. "Promise you'll turn me back on?"

"Andy, we've been all through this before. Of course I will. I promise."

"It's kind of like dying, you know."

"No. It's more like going to sleep. No one knows what dying's like."

"But I can't wake up by myself like you can. I have to depend on you to do it for me. What if you forgot?"

"I won't forget. You know that. How long have we been working together now?"

"Four years, two months, six days, and, uh . . . seven hours, twenty minutes, and forty-two seconds—not counting the leap second three years ago."

"Very funny, pal. Now be quiet, you're going to sleep."

Taylor tabbed a few commands onto the keyboard, and Andy closed his eyes. The computer gathered more than seventeen terabytes of data from Andrew's systems, analyzed the database, and downloaded the results.

Taylor labeled the data by keying in Andy's full name, Andrew D. Roid, along with the location, date, and time. He searched the output for any flags. Nothing out of range, no error codes. He tabbed in the command to awaken Andy, who opened his eyes without a trace of grogginess.

"You're perfect!" Taylor said.

"Of course."

"Okay, Andy, shirt back on," Taylor said, pulling the plug. "You ready for the big day tomorrow? You know two of our top execs will be observing; Senior Directors Moira Lambert and Jerome Mosby are here."

"I'm a little nervous, but that's a good thing. Kind of like butterflies before a performance, huh?"

Taylor turned aside to make an entry into his computer, a slight frown on his face. "Yeah, Andy, all the astronauts and specialists get a case of the nerves before a flight test simulation, even you, Mr. Perfection," he lied. "Hop down, and let's get you home."

Taylor led Andy back to a sterile, climate-controlled enclosure with padded restraints and strapped him in much like a crew chief buckling in a NASCAR driver. Once secured he said, "Time to go to sleep, Andy. I'll waken you in time to get ready for the simulation tomorrow."

Taylor avoided using the term "hibernate" because it was too inhuman. A few moments after Taylor powered him down, Andy shut his eyes. Taylor closed the lid of the compartment and locked it. He left the lab, shaking his head. *Andy shouldn't be exhibiting nervousness*, he thought.

The Ares I crew consisted of four members. Andrew served as the capsule commander and had the responsibility for all flight operations and maneuvers. Pilot Brady Owen, second in command, backed up the commander and would perform his duties if necessary. Mission Specialist Ashlyn Johnson, one of a set of identical twins, had the job of operating the Higgs-Boson equipment on board. And Mission Specialist Taylor Carson provided technical support for the android.

Andrew and Brady had spent the morning with the flight director poring over pages of operational and emergency procedures and repeating them from memory until they were letter perfect. The portion of the mission scheduled to be simulated was the most critical segment of the entire trip. After entering a Martian orbit in tandem with Phobos and launching a probe to the potato-shaped moon's surface, the Ares I vehicle was to perform a slingshot maneuver around Mars. The vehicle would use the red planet's gravitational field to provide a boost to the capsule for the return flight to Earth. There could be no errors, for the slightest deviation could either cause the capsule to crash on the Martian surface or send it careening into deep space.

The flight director closed the session and dismissed the two pilots once he was satisfied with their knowledge and responses. Grabbing a sandwich from his lunch bag, he took a big bite and wolfed it down. "Send in Taylor and Ashlyn," he said, between bites. "I want to go over the procedures for the mission specialists during the slingshot."

Andrew left the room looking as crisp and bright as he did when he arrived, but Brady appeared weary and disheveled, his shirt bathed in sweat. They met the two mission specialists waiting in the anteroom.

"Your turn in the barrel," Brady said, nodding his head back toward the small conference room. "Be forewarned. He's on a real tirade today."

Neither pilot would participate in the second session since the focus would be on the roles of the specialists.

Taylor rushed Andrew to his storage compartment and packed him inside. Ignoring the pleading look on Andrew's face, Taylor placed the android in hibernation and closed the compartment door. Trying to avoid the ire of the already aggravated flight director, Taylor sprinted back to the meeting and grabbed a seat next to Ashlyn. He opened his operations manual and thumbed to the page that had been whispered to him by Ashlyn. The flight director looked up from his manual and glared over his reading glasses at Taylor. "About time you joined us," he said.

"Sorry, I had to put Andrew up," Taylor said. "He can't be left—"

"Never mind the excuses," the flight director said, cutting him off. "Let's pick it up from here and go on. I don't want to have to start over."

Working through page after page of the timeline, the specialists demonstrated to the flight director that they had the procedures down cold. When they finished, the flight director made a shocking statement:

"I split this readiness review into two segments because I want to alert you to something the pilots won't be told—and for the purpose of a successful simulation, it has to be kept confidential."

Taylor couldn't believe his ears. Why would the flight director keep information from the pilots, yet reveal it to the specialists who were regarded by most as being merely a step above passengers along for the ride.

The flight director continued. "The instant before initiating the burn to begin the sling shot maneuver, we're going to cut the power to Andrew and prevent the solenoid relays from switching him to his internal backup battery power."

Taylor dropped his pen in surprise. Gathering himself, he said, "I can't agree with doing that. It could be disastrous."

"We have to verify the ability for a human to take over in the event we lose Andrew. We need to be sure there are no hitches. If so, it is better we find them out during a simulation rather than in deep space. The simulator won't crash if something bad happens. What's your concern?"

Taylor remained silent, wondering whether he should state his issue and risk a mission delay or even a cancellation. He opted to speak.

"Because of his command responsibilities, we programmed Andrew's thought and deductive reasoning algorithms to make his artificial intelligence capabilities as close to human thought processes as possible. He learns from his mistakes and continually improves his decision making."

The director didn't blink. "You're not telling me anything I don't know."

Taylor slowly exhaled and continued, "We even ignored the so-called three laws of robotics: 1) a robot may not harm a human; 2) a robot must obey orders given it by a human—unless they would cause it to violate the first law; and 3) a robot must protect its own existence as long as that does not violate the first two laws. We didn't implant these laws because humans are not constrained by them, and Andrew had to be as human as possible. He's in command for most of the en route portion of the trip while the others are either sedated or tending to other duties or needs."

"Are you going to answer my question, or are you going to continue to lecture me on things I already know?"

Ashlyn's body language showed she was uncomfortable with the blunt response.

Taylor swallowed and revealed his concern. "I've seen indications that we've been successful, perhaps too much so. Andrew is developing a self-awareness. He's a bit nervous about the simulation tomorrow."

"I'm not surprised by that."

"Today, he associated being turned off with dying. Nothing major yet, but if we turn him off during the most critical phase of the simulation, he may wake with a sense of failure, coupled with a loss of self-confidence—a most important attribute for the commander of a capsule in deep space where round trip communications with Mission Control take forty minutes. Your test may wreck him as a commander."

"Taylor, I'm afraid you're becoming too close to Andrew, almost his buddy. Again, I'll say, if it is to happen, better it happens during a simulation when lives are not at risk. We're going ahead as planned."

Taylor started to object, but thought better of it and acquiesced to the director's statement. When the session ended, Taylor returned to the room where he had stored Andy to file his notes on the simulation. He turned to leave but the lock on the door of Andy's enclosure caught his attention. A surge of adrenaline caused his heart to race.

It's unlocked, he thought. *I could swear I locked it.* He opened the enclosure door in a state of panic. His apprehension subsided when he saw Andy still in place, asleep. *Can't believe I did that*, he thought. *Someone could have stolen a billion dollar machine vital to the success of our mission.* This time when he closed the door, he made certain he locked it.

The next morning, clad in her robe and slippers, Moira sipped the second cup of coffee she had brewed from the pot in their hotel room, trying to brush the cobwebs from her mind before attending her briefing on the simulation later that day. So far, the coffee wasn't working. *I'm getting too old for this*, she thought. *Should have gotten a good night's rest.* She glanced at Crawford, sprawled on the bed, fast asleep, with the covers half askew. Smiling, Moira entertained the thought of crawling back into bed with him for a bit before getting ready. *Nope, I'd just start something I don't have time to finish.*

The ringtone of her phone interrupted her thoughts. She tried to answer it before the noise awakened her husband. "Hello."

"Moira Lambert?" the caller asked.

"Yes."

"The NASA Administrator has called an emergency conference. You're requested to be in the board room in thirty minutes."

The shock broke over Moira. Her first reaction was a concern about the mission. "Do you know the topic?" she asked.

"All I am permitted to say is that it's about the Russian space probe, *Fobos 5*. You need to hurry."

Chapter Two – *Fobos 5*

No time for a morning shower, Moira opted for a bird bath instead, dampening her washcloth in the basin of the sink. She brushed her teeth and scrambled to get dressed. As she applied her makeup, Crawford approached her from behind, placed his hands on her shoulders, and kissed her on the nape of her neck. Moira placed her own hand on one of his, restraining him from going further. "Can't, sweetheart, got a call to come in for an emergency meeting."

"Anything serious?" Crawford asked.

"Don't know, but I suspect it may be a problem for the Russians. Something to do with their current probe, *Fobos 5,* that's approaching Phobos."

"I think that little moon has the Ruskies jinxed. They've been plagued with catastrophes trying to land there. Good thing their missions have all been unmanned. Maybe the rumors about Phobos being an extraterrestrial satellite have some basis in truth."

Moira reached for her brush and began doing her hair. She pooh-poohed his comment. "You've been reading too many urban legends. Phobos is a tiny, captured asteroid, that's all. Nothing more, so don't go all conspiratorial on me."

Crawford poured himself a cup of coffee and sat in a chair next to hers. He didn't give up.

"So why is NASA so interested in Phobos, then? Isn't one of your mission objectives to determine if it *is* extraterrestrial?"

"Our primary objective is to begin the process of establishing a base on Phobos for the purpose of staging future missions that will land on Mars. We'll stockpile fuel, equipment, and supplies at the base to reduce the payload requirement for the later missions that will descend to the Martian surface and return—like the Lunar Module did for our Apollo moon landings."

"But isn't another objective to prove whether or not it is extraterrestrial?"

Moira stood, straightened her jacket and checked her appearance in the mirror. "It is. But only because of the public interest in the matter. Adding that objective helped us secure funding for the whole Ares program. Believe me, we don't think there are little green men on Phobos."

"I'm not so sure that the Russians don't. They keep trying even though they've lost several spacecraft. I still think there's something eerie going on. Those two moons, Phobos and Deimos—what was it they were named for?" Crawford asked. "Oh yeah, I remember now—fear and terror. Well, from what I've heard, I wouldn't want to be trying to land on either one of them. The Russians certainly have had bad luck."

Moira knew all the history. The Russians had lost contact with three of their previous *Fobos* series probes: *Fobos 1* and *Fobos 2* in the 1980s and *Fobos 3* in 2011. Never learning the true cause for the losses, the Russians had, among other possibilities, implicated the U.S. as being complicit in a conspiracy theory to protect U.S. interests.

Ten years after losing *Fobos 3*, the Russians launched *Fobos 4*, designed to perform extensive mineralogy mapping of the satellite and to return soil samples from its surface. That mission proved to be successful, but Russia never made public any information the probe gathered. As a result of their findings, however, Russia redoubled its efforts to probe the tiny moon, and *Fobos 5* was a much larger probe with several cargo bays. Rumors persisted that the Russians planned to land equipment on Phobos in preparation for a manned expedition to follow.

Her thoughts returned to the emergency meeting. *What's happened to Fobos 5?* Moira wondered. She rushed for the door and blew Crawford a kiss as she departed.

In a room adjacent to the simulator in Building 9, crew member Ashlyn Johnson finished zipping up her space suit with the assistance of two technicians. Although the test today was a simulation, the crew would be in full gear, including their helmets. All the biometric sensors were in place, held by adhesive patches like those for an electrocardiogram. Ashlyn squirmed in an attempt to relieve the tension on a couple of the patches that were too tight, causing some discomfort. To no avail. *Just have to put up with them*, she sighed. *It's only for one day—not for a whole year on the actual round-trip flight.*

Brady Owen, helmet still in hand, smiled when she had finished. "We'll be able to take the suits off during the flight, once we're out of our orbit around Earth."

Ashlyn nodded, checking the clock to see how much longer it would be before they could walk to the simulator, board, and strap in. *Not too long*, she thought, trying to keep her mind off the thought of going to the bathroom. No provisions for that during this simulation, except to use her suit, and she didn't want to join the club of astronauts who had done that.

A technician opened the door, and said, "If everyone's ready, let's go."

Ashlyn stood, welcoming the invitation. Brady donned his helmet, and a technician twisted it a few degrees to lock it in place. Once satisfied with the security of Brady's helmet, the technician turned to Ashlyn and Taylor and helped them lock their own. Ashlyn walked with an awkward gait beside Brady and Taylor into the huge lab, and as always, the sight of the capsule mockup created an overwhelming sense of awe within her. One hundred feet in length and eighteen feet in diameter, it stretched from wall to wall. Consisting of four major sections, the assembly was emblazoned with a huge "USA" and the Ares I mission logo. Power supply lines, oxygen and water hoses, and numerous sensor and data cords connected to various points on the simulator and crisscrossed the floor of the lab, creating a chaotic look to an otherwise image of engineering perfection. The hum of ancillary equipment in the lab made talking difficult and a distinct aroma of ozone irritated the linings of the nostrils of the people inside.

Technicians led the three of them to the scissors-lift to board the capsule, steadying them with helpful hands.

One tech said. "We'll get Brady on board first and strap him into the pilot's seat. Ashlyn, we'll take you next and seat you behind Brady. Taylor, you're after her, on her left. Once you're all secure, we'll put Andy in the commander's seat."

Ashlyn entered the capsule and struggled with her bulky suit to reach her seat, situated on the far side in the second row behind the pilot. Next to her was the complex arrangement of the Higgs-Boson equipment provided by Japan. Developed under the direction of Kazuhiro Sora, the president of H-B Enterprises, the equipment had a twofold purpose. One was to analyze some peculiar surface anomalies on Phobos in an attempt to determine how long they had been in existence, and second, to amplify the extrasensory communications abilities of Ashlyn and her twin, Jaelyn, across the miles of deep space.

Ashlyn had spent years with her twin working with Kazuhiro on the project's development and knew the equipment's capabilities and idiosyncrasies better than anyone besides Kazuhiro himself.

Taylor struggled to wedge himself into his seat. Once in place, the technicians strapped him in, one of them stomping heavily on his shoulder to make certain the belt could be cinched tight. "Damn it, man, don't be so rough," Taylor said, wincing from pain.

"Sorry," the tech said. "We can't have you floating around when the main engines are ignited."

"That's not going to be today."

"From now on, the simulation's real," the tech said. "I've stomped on every astronaut since the Apollo days. It's kind of like a good luck ritual. Welcome to the club!"

"Thanks, buddy—I think!"

Andy turned to greet each of them. "Hi, guys, welcome aboard!"

"Where's *your* suit and helmet?" Ashlyn teased, her voice muffled by her own helmet.

"Oops! Left it at the cleaners," Andy said. "I'm on a diet, too. I've given up air, water, and food."

"Cut it out, you old bucket of bolts and scrap wire, or I'll pull your plug. We'll see how funny you can be then," Brady said, elbowing Andy in his side.

"Not a speck of rust. No wrinkles or baggy eyes. No splotches. Still have a full head of hair and unlike some humans, I look as good as the day I was born."

"Activated," Brady said, correcting him.

"*Born.*"

"Stop it, you two," Ashlyn said. "We've got a big job to do."

Once the lighthearted banter stopped, Ashlyn resigned herself to the two-hour wait while Andy and Brady powered up the simulator and programmed it for the day's mission. She allowed her mind to visit her favorite place of beauty and calm, the misty shoreline of the Olympic Peninsula. Her thoughts would remain there until her scheduled duties were to begin. Taylor spent the time worrying about what might happen with Andy later in the simulation.

★ ★ ★

Moira entered the NASA boardroom and took a seat in one of the leather swivel chairs. She greeted the other senior directors, making apologies for being a few minutes late. "Houston traffic," she said, not wanting to confide in the men present that she never went in public without her appearance being perfect. They needn't know it had taken her a few extra minutes to dig through her luggage and find the red belt she had packed for the occasion. She noticed a couple of the men present still had a morning shadow and one had on a rumpled shirt.

Not professional, she thought. *And poor judgment.*

No sooner had she taken her seat than did the video screen in the front of the room come to life. It projected the image of NASA Administrator Robert Durand with a stern expression on his face. Not wasting a second on amenities, Administrator Durand spoke in measured terms.

"We received word less than an hour ago from the Department of Defense that Russia lost contact with its latest probe, *Fobos 5*. It was within minutes of reaching a Martian orbit in tandem with Phobos."

A few gasps were heard around the table. None could fathom another occasion for a Russian failure.

Durand continued speaking. "I must make you aware of a critical development: Russia, in releasing information about this loss, is blaming the U.S. for a reason that's incomprehensible. They are saying we know something about Phobos that we do not want shared with the public. Through private, high-level diplomatic channels, they are accusing us of having discovered that Phobos is an artificial satellite and that we are keeping it quiet to avoid a major panic."

Durand's expression remained stoic, giving no clue to his reaction to the Russian allegations. After a few moments of silence, the Phobos mission director raised the question all were thinking. "What impact will this have on our mission?"

"Until we have reason to do otherwise, we're going ahead as planned. Our public affairs department is preparing a release stating our sincere regrets for the Russian misfortune, thankful that the probe was unmanned with no loss of life, but not mentioning anything else. Continue with your work, but remain wary. Remember, the Russians have now lost four out of their five probes, and we don't know the reason for those losses. Our own mission could be vulnerable to the same danger, whatever it might be, but unlike Russia, we will have human lives at stake. We will keep you advised of any pertinent developments."

The administrator's image on the screen shrank to a small, oscillating circle of white light before the screen faded to black.

Chapter Three – Higgs-Boson

Moira hurried from the board room to a suite adjacent to the NASA cafeteria for a private luncheon meeting with Kazuhiro Sora to discuss the status of the Higgs-Boson experiment scheduled for Ares I. She had met Kazuhiro more than ten years ago when she negotiated with his Japanese company for a science exchange.

The trade involved swapping NASA heavy-lift booster technology for the knowledge Kazuhiro had gained from his work with the Higgs-Boson particle, more commonly known as the "God Particle," a sub-atomic particle discovered by the Hadron Collider in Great Britain. The particle traveled at nearly the speed of light and in so doing, created mass within the nucleus of the atom. This creation was likened to that of God, hence the nickname—loved by the media, but loathed by scientists.

A particular area of focus in Kazuhiro's work concerned the energy field generated by the particle. Like a magnetic field, the Higgs-Boson field extended indefinitely. Since all matter, including human cells, contained the particles, the field served to interconnect all things—even across time. Kazuhiro's initial work led to the development of a primitive ansible, a device that could communicate to a receiver in a different time period.

His company, H-B Enterprises, had refined the science and developed equipment—now on board Ares I—that could scan an object and determine when it originated. Unlike carbon dating, the H-B Analyzer didn't have to come into contact with an object to provide results. Nor did it require the object to have a carbon base. It could analyze the age of granite as easily as a tree trunk.

Through the years, Moira had extensive dealings with Kazuhiro and his company. No longer wary competitors, they had become close friends who valued each other's talents.

Moira rose when Kazuhiro entered the room and returned his bow before offering him an enthusiastic hand shake. She smiled at his appearance. Dressed in a three-piece, pinstriped business suit, he still wore his prized Stetson and ostrich boots Moira had given him on behalf of NASA as part of the initial negotiation proceedings. Kazuhiro loved visiting Texas and enjoyed its cuisine, particularly its Texas-sized steaks rubbed with jalapeno flavored sauces.

Such a petite, courteous man with a humongous appetite. Wonder if he's ordered steak for lunch, she thought. *He'd move from L.A. to Texas if it were at all possible for him.*

"Good morning, Ms. Rambert," he said, greeting her with his familiar tease.

"*Lambert,*" Moira said, responding as usual.

"I know," he said, with a big grin. "Just kidding."

The greeting between the two of them had never gotten old. For all the immense scientific ability Kazuhiro had mastered, his sense of humor made him down to earth and likeable. He removed his hat, revealing a shoulder-length, bushy head of gray hair, perhaps a nod to Einstein or even an indicator of his free-spirited, alter ego. He set the hat on a vacant chair seat, upside down to preserve the natural roll of the brim.

Moira offered him a seat at the table and without hesitating, jumped to business. "We've got to be in the simulator observation room in less than an hour, so we're short on time. Is your analyzer going to be ready when it comes time for the actual mission?"

"It will be ready by the time your probe has been assembled at the ISS. We're ahead of schedule," Kazuhiro said.

He was referencing NASA's plan for the sections of the Ares I probe to be carried to the ISS—the International Space Station—in four different flights and assembled in space. NASA had been forced to abandon its original plan to launch a vehicle from the surface of the Earth, due to a need to develop a launch vehicle far more powerful than the three-stage, Saturn 5 behemoths that propelled the Apollo moon missions into space. Several catastrophic failures of the new engines during test firings at the John C. Stennis Space Center in Mississippi caused NASA—under immense public pressure—to switch to an alternate strategy.

Instead of launching the entire spacecraft from the Earth's surface with mammoth rocket engines, a modular craft was designed with components that would be individually lifted to the space station with much smaller rockets. At the station, the components would be assembled, and the spacecraft would be launched from there with its own propulsion system.

The alternate plan used an innovative Photon Sail to accelerate the vehicle on the outbound segment so that the weight and fuel requirements for the mission could be greatly reduced. The vehicle would make the return trip home by using the gravity of Mars as a slingshot and then firing its engines with the remaining fuel to accelerate homeward.

"So you're confident that your H-B Analyzer can accurately date the surface anomalies on Phobos?" Moira asked, referring to the enigmatic structures the second Russian probe had photographed before data transmission had been lost.

"We've tested it on Earth objects from a satellite. It correctly dated the major mountain ranges—the Rockies, the Alps, and even the Himalayas. But—"

"But what?"

"We had to throw out some readings on ancient structures. The data on Stonehenge and the Pyramids were puzzling and inconclusive."

"Inconclusive? You're beginning to worry me."

"We expected the structures to be five- to ten-thousand-years old. But our analyzer showed them to be more than 200-million-years old."

"You probably were getting readings on the granite."

"No, the analyzer doesn't date an object that way," Kazuhiro reminded her. He held his hands in front of him at eye level, thumbs together and palms facing her, like a movie director might do when framing a shot. "It scans an object in the present and provides an 'after' picture—except it isn't a picture, it's a Higgs-Boson field signature pattern of complex lines and colors. Then we scan the same image back through time until the computer detects a change in the pattern. That becomes the 'before' picture and tells us when the change took place."

The wait staff interrupted their conversation by bringing their lunch and placing it on their table.

Moira marveled at how quickly Kazuhiro began devouring his steak. *Sixteen ounces, and he'll finish it before I'm done with my salad. Glad he's having a light lunch, or he would have ordered a larger one!*

Between bites, Moira asked the tough question. "So our science experiment that will be on board Ares I may provide inconclusive results, too?"

"It's a possibility. But it's also possible that Stonehenge and the Pyramids are as old as our analyzer says they are."

"Kazuhiro, if there's anything you can do to validate your analyzer in the next eight months before our mission launches, I'm asking you to do so. We are risking three human lives to obtain a correct answer. We must have confidence in the results we get."

"Ms. Lambert, I will do everything I can, but a degree of uncertainty is always present in experimental science."

Moira's cell phone reminded her the time had come to depart for the simulation. Kazuhiro donned his hat and walked with her to the door of the suite and to the tram waiting for them. Moira's lunch had not settled well on her stomach.

Chapter Four – Simulation

A small crowd of tourists, led by a NASA guide, took their seats behind a plate glass window in a room overlooking the simulator. The members of the group ranged from college students knowledgeable about the NASA program, to men happy to get out of the heat and sit in a comfortable seat, and to moms struggling with toddlers—some half asleep, some screaming, and others with chocolate ice cream smeared over their cheeks and dripping onto their clothes. All were weary from the amount of walking they had experienced on the morning tour.

A young woman at the front of the room, wearing NASA's classic blue jumpsuit and a cap with her golden-brown pony tail protruding through the rear band, encouraged the visitors to take their seats. "Good afternoon. I'm Jaelyn Johnson, a mission specialist in the Ares program. We have a few minutes before the simulation starts," she said. "Let me brief you on the program."

All but a few gave her their attention. She stepped to the center of the window and faced them. "NASA's Ares program, identified by the original name the Greeks gave to what we now call Mars, is a series of scheduled manned missions to that planet," she said. "In all of the world's history of space travel, no probe has yet taken humans into deep space and brought them back. It's a daunting task. To carry enough fuel for the return trip, the Ares vehicles will be launched from the International Space Station, after they have been assembled there and satisfactorily passed exhaustive pre-flight tests. Once out of Earth orbit, the vehicles will accelerate to their en route velocity using one of the most ancient propulsion systems—a sail."

Jaelyn paused for a moment to let that surprise soak in. She glanced at several people in her audience to determine if they were following her. She continued. "Except this sail is not made from canvas, it is a revolutionary, hi-tech, electronics grid that captures the solar wind, an array of photons emanating from the sun. The grid, more than one mile in diameter, is composed of a labyrinth of gossamer strands, similar to those in a spider web, that are electrically energized. Like opposing magnets, the photons push against the sail and propel the craft. Once the capsule attains an orbit in tandem with Phobos, the sail will be jettisoned and the return trip will be made using traditional rocket engine power."

Jaelyn could see that a few people in her audience understood the concept and were fascinated by it. Others, however, accepted the notion as a matter of course and were more worried about lunch than the science behind the missions.

"On this first expedition to the tiny Martian moon, Phobos, the crew will scan the satellite's surface with special equipment to provide a map of the terrain. In addition, an unmanned probe will land on Phobos and sample the soil's composition and stability. During the next three missions, crews will establish a base on the moon's surface and stock it with fuel and supplies. On the last four missions, crews will use a special landing vehicle to descend from the base to the Martian surface for exploration. While they are gone, the Ares vehicle will remain parked in orbit along with its android commander. Finally the crews will return to the Ares vehicle to slingshot around Mars and gain a velocity boost for the return to Earth."

A student raised a hand. Jaelyn nodded. "Why not descend to Mars directly from a Martian orbit instead of landing on Phobos?"

"Good question. The vehicle assembly and propulsion mechanism would be way too complex to accomplish the mission in that manner. We need to use Phobos as a base and stage our landings from there. Even then, it will take eight missions to accomplish our objectives."

"Is that the actual Ares I vehicle we see down there?" one of the teens asked.

"No, it is a simulator, designed to train the crew for the first mission. Today's task will be for the crew to enter an orbit in tandem with Phobos and perform the slingshot maneuver around Mars to return home. This sequence is critical to the success of the entire expedition, and it must be conducted by the crew without the oversight and assistance of Mission Control due to the forty-minute delay in communications caused by the enormous distances involved."

One of the women, cradling a toddler on her lap, asked a question. "Who are those people gathering in the room across from us?"

Jaelyn looked around. "We have some VIPs observing the simulation today. The lady is Senior Director Moira Lambert, whose organization has the responsibility for the science experiments on board. Next to her is Kazuhiro Sora, the president of H-B Enterprises, who has developed the science equipment. I also see the Senior Director for the NASA Missions Division, Jerome Mosby, who has the overall flight responsibility for the Ares program."

One little boy popped out of his seat and stood in front of the window. "Who's the astronaut getting in who is not wearing a space suit? He's just got a golf shirt on."

Jaelyn laughed. "That, my observant little friend, is Andy, and he's an android. He'll be flying the ship most of the time—the crew will be more than six months en route—and he never gets tired. We couldn't fly the mission without him."

"What's his last name?"

"It's 'Roid.' Say his name for me."

"Andy."

"Both names."

"Andy Roid."

"Again. Over and over—faster."

"Andy Roid—Andy Roid—Andyroi . . . oh! I get it—Android!"

"That's right!"

"Cool!"

"While I'm at it, let me introduce the other members of the crew. The pilot is Brady Owen, Taylor Carson is a mission specialist, and the woman is my twin sister, Ashlyn. We've been working together for two years on the H-B experiment, but she lucked out and got the first mission. I won't be going until the fourth."

Jaelyn leaned next to the little boy and whispered. "I'll tell you a secret, if you won't tell anyone. Andy's a close buddy of my boyfriend, Taylor."

The little boy pressed his face against the glass and waved. "Hi, Andy," he said.

As circumstance would have it, Andy glanced up through the hatch just in time to see the boy wave. He offered a big wave and smile in return. The little boy jumped up and down, squealing with excitement.

"Okay, everyone, let's watch for a few minutes," Jaelyn said. "I see that they are closing the hatch."

Jaelyn breathed a sigh of relief, thankful this time that no one brought up the question about the possibility of Phobos being an artificial satellite, placed in orbit by extraterrestrials eons ago. Jaelyn had heard it all. From the opinion of noted astronomer and author, Carl Sagan, based on his calculations, that Phobos was a metallic, hollow object and thus artificial, all the way to Buzz Aldrin's contention that an obelisk on the surface of Phobos served as evidence of extraterrestrial life and we needed to send a probe to solve the mystery.

Even the Russians were part of the enigma. Their second probe, *Fobos 2*, launched in 1988, took pictures of a city-like grid on the satellite's surface. The last complete picture showed an elliptical shadow that some believe could have been made by a huge UFO. The Russians were in the process of taking an additional photograph when they lost communications with the probe. They never released that partial photograph, but there were persistent rumors it showed an alien craft approaching the probe.

One of the scientists at the Russian Space Research Institute lost his job after speaking publicly about the probe and saying that "it had been knocked out of orbit and was spiraling out of control."

Thank God, I didn't have to deal with any of that today, she thought.

Jaelyn had not yet heard the news that the most recent Russian probe, *Fobos 5*, had been lost and that the Russians were accusing the U.S. of being responsible for its loss, supposedly to cover up knowledge the government held about Phobos being artificial.

Two people sat across from each other at a small table in a dim corner of the bar, and the younger of the two appeared to become nervous when questioned by the other. "Did you get it done?"

"No," he answered in a hushed tone, not facing his questioner.

"Why not? We had it all set up. What happened?"

"I got the compartment unlocked using the code you gave me. That part of it worked fine," he said. "But—"

"Damn you. There were to be no 'buts.' Go on."

"Before I could open the compartment door, some NASA guy barged into the room. To keep from being caught, I dove underneath a table and stayed there until he left."

"Do you think he suspected anything?"

A long pause.

"I don't think so. The NASA guy opened the door and appeared to be relieved when he saw the droid undisturbed. I think he thought the unlocked door was due to his own forgetfulness. Then he left."

"Why didn't you finish the job?"

"The code didn't work when I tried it again. When I entered it, an error message showed on the display above the lock: 'ENTRY NOT ACCEPTED.' I think the guy changed the code just to be sure."

The other man glared at the first. "It'll take us weeks to gain the new information and get set up to try again. At least it doesn't look like our cover has been blown. Stay low. I'll contact you when we're ready. Give me the device."

The younger man looked around to be certain they were not being observed. He reached into his jacket pocket and withdrew a small box. He placed it on the table and slid it to the other who slipped it into his briefcase and said, "You leave first. I'll stay here to double check that you're not being followed. Go about your work as normal until you hear from me."

Once the younger man left, the other waited a few minutes, watching for anyone who might be tailing his associate. Satisfied, he grabbed his Stetson and walked through the bar and stepped into the muggy outside heat.

Moira watched the final preparations being made for the simulation. She had a lot resting on the success of this session—and even more on the Ares program. Her Science Division had the responsibility for the development of three major components of the mission. First, of course, was Andrew's software decision-making algorithms, second was the Higgs-Boson equipment, and third, the one-mile-diameter electronic grid of the sail that was to power the deep-space probe outbound using the energy from the solar wind. Human lives were at stake along with a spacecraft costing close to a trillion dollars.

Her stomach churned with nervousness. It didn't help that seated next to her was Senior Director Jerome Mosby, her prime competitor for the NASA Administrator's job when the present administrator retired in two years. If the program were successful, they would compete on an equal footing. But if either one failed in their responsibilities, the other would become the leading candidate.

No turning back, now, Moira thought. She offered Kazuhiro Sora a seat next to her with a smile and a slight bow of her head.

"Thank you, Rambert," he said, bowing with his usual grin.

"My pleasure, Kazuhiro."

Jerome leaned toward the two of them and spoke. "We're five minutes away from the simulation step to perform the burn that will begin the slingshot maneuver. They just uploaded the details from Mission Control."

Above the viewing window were two monitors, one projecting an over-the-shoulder look at the occupants of the command module and the other showing a view of the controllers directing the simulation.

Moira watched as Andrew punched in the burn parameters. With no warning, the android dropped his arms and slumped back in his seat. He did not respond to Brady Owen's frantic attempts to rouse him. Taylor reached forward with the thought of helping Andrew but decided against it. *It's a planned test,* he thought. *Control wants to see how Brady handles the emergency.*

"Control, we have an issue. Switching to emergency procedure." Due to the simulated time lag, Control could not answer. Brady tabbed in the correct procedure and began to follow in sequence the steps portrayed on the command panel in front of him.

Brady knew Control would take nearly forty minutes to respond because of the time it took for the transmission to travel the sixty million miles to Earth and return—even at the speed of light. This extensive time lag required the crew to be self-reliant and handle emergencies without being dependent on Mission Control as were the crews for the moon shots. Each Ares I crew member had been trained to back up another member's position. Brady knew he was on his own and called for Ashlyn to read aloud each step of the procedure so that he could implement it on the timeline required.

"Initiate retro burn on my mark," Ashlyn called.

Brady lifted the guard above the switch and positioned his fingertip above it.

"Mark!"

Brady triggered the switch, and they both were pressed forward in their seat by the deceleration. A digital timer popped up on the screen and counted down toward zero.

At the instant the counter reached zero, Brady snapped the switch off. He switched the screen display to one that depicted the capsule's progress along an ideal track with parallel bands that showed permissible variation.

"Velocity and track is nominal," Brady said. "We are in orbit around Mars. In fifty minutes we'll ignite the main engines for the burn to break free from Mars and put us on our trajectory to Earth. Stay alert. I'll see if I can reboot Andy."

The monitors in the viewing room showed the drama in real time. Moira could not believe her worst nightmare had come true. Andrew had suffered a failure and only the quick and correct actions by the humans on board had prevented a disaster. She glanced at Jerome, half expecting him to gloat, but instead he had a smile on his face.

"Don't worry, Ms. Lambert," he said, "we programmed an unannounced failure into the android to check the ability of the crew to manage the crisis. I gave instructions that only those who had a need to know were informed in advance. Sorry."

"I should have been made aware," Moira said. "You took a big risk. We still don't know what impact this situation will have on Andrew. It could render him unfit for the actual mission."

"We weighed that possibility and determined the risk was worth it. We know the droid can perform the slingshot maneuver, but we had to be certain our astronaut and specialists could step in and handle an emergency. Looks like they passed our test without missing a beat."

"I disagree with your approach. We'll discuss this further." Moira focused her attention back on the command module monitor.

Brady had disconnected Andrew's umbilical cord and opened a concealed panel within his chest. A circuit board displayed a red light, and Brady reset that board to its default parameters. Reconnecting the umbilical cord, Brady rebooted Andrew, who awoke and scanned the control panel. In an instant, he saw time had passed and several steps had been taken with him being unaware. "What happened?" he asked.

Brady told Andrew that he had been disabled for a few minutes as part of the simulation to see how the crew responded to his loss.

Not happy about being part of an experiment, Andy resumed command without hesitation. "Main engines burn in seventeen minutes, twenty-one seconds. We're headed home!"

Brady relaxed. He felt he had responded well to the emergency and was all too happy to let Andrew take over again. The android appeared to suffer no residual effects of his failure.

Once the capsule had been inserted into the return-to-Earth trajectory, Control concluded the simulation. Moira and the others filed out of the viewing room.

Except for Moira's concern for Andrew, all parties were happy with the simulation—the crew, the controllers, and all the technicians associated with the test. When Jerome exited the room and entered the hallway, however, the flight director buttonholed him.

Jerome clapped him on the back and congratulated him for the success. "The simulation went well," he said, complimenting him.

The flight director grasped Jerome's elbow and held him back from the others. "It went too well," he said. "The failure of the android was not something we had rehearsed. Nor did we review it in our readiness review. Brady called up the correct emergency procedure and enacted it step by step without blinking an eye. I think someone tipped Andrew off. He knew what was coming and might have helped Brady be on the alert for it."

"Who the hell could be guilty of leaking that information?"

The flight director whispered, "Who is Andrew's buddy?"

"You mean Taylor?"

"Who else could have done it?"

"Ms. Lambert and I are going to have a serious talk. Her organization can't get even the fundamentals right, and the incompetence of her people, Taylor in particular, pose a risk to the safety of the mission. I'm going to take that ambitious bitch down a notch."

★ ★ ★

Taylor and Andrew walked out of the simulation lab in the company of the other two crew members who were chatting about the success of the simulation. Andrew, however, appeared to be in a down mood. Before Taylor could ask him about it, Brady interrupted with an invitation.

"Ashlyn and I are going to meet some friends and celebrate with a few drinks at the Interstellar Club," Brady said. "You'll come with us, won't you, Taylor?"

"Love to," Taylor said. "You two go on ahead. I'll be there just as soon as I get Andy put up."

"Don't be too long," Ashlyn said. "Jaelyn's going with us. You wouldn't want her to meet up with some hunk, would you?"

"You mean some *other* hunk?"

"Yeah, right! But you know single women get lots of company at the club."

"I'll be there," Taylor said. He turned to Andrew and gave him a fist bump. "Good work today, Andy! Come on, let's go home."

The two separated from the others and walked toward the storage room. Andrew lagged behind.

"What's the matter, pal?" Taylor asked.

"Nothing really, but—"

"But what? You did great today. Why so glum?"

Andrew stopped. He looked back to be sure they were alone.

"I don't feel good about what we did today. You know—me telling Brady what was coming after you let me in on the secret."

"Hey, Andy. You let me worry about that."

"It was sort of like . . . uh, cheating, wasn't it?"

"Where on earth did you get an idea like that?"

"We weren't supposed to know. Maybe we kept the controllers from learning something important—maybe even something that would save the real mission."

Taylor realized the android was dealing with a sense of guilt— another human trait. He tried to put a different perspective on Andrew's mindset. "Andy, we know an astronaut has to be prepared for any contingency. They must prepare themselves so thoroughly that there are no surprises. The mission depends upon that. Keep that in mind. You didn't cheat, but you were prepared. Today, you demonstrated that you were ready for any possibility— that's all. Knock off the damned guilt trip."

They neared the door to the storage room. Before Taylor could open it, Andrew put his hand on the knob and stared at Taylor.

"And there's another thing," Andrew said. "All the rest of you are going out to party, but me—who has the responsibility for the success of the mission—well, what's my reward? Guess what? I get to go back into my box. It pisses me off. I don't like it in there."

"Andy, you're being an ass," Taylor said. "You know you can't go with us."

"Why not? Just once I'd like to have a good time. Hell, you never know. I might even like to dance with some girl. Maybe Jaelyn, since you're always so preoccupied taking care of Robo-boy."

"*Robo*-boy? Andy, you are a superb commander—there's none better. But you'd be lost in the real world, particularly in some singles bar. Besides, we couldn't risk anything happening to a billion dollar piece of equipment. Not in some bar, anyway," Taylor said, getting frustrated with Andy's insolence.

"Piece of equipment. Is that what you think of me? Some expensive toy to be put away when you're tired of playing?"

"Come on, Andy, you know better than that. Let me open the door."

"Only if you promise to take me with you some day—I mean it."

Taylor and Andrew stared at each other, each waiting for the other to back down. After a few moments, the standoff became uncomfortable.

Taylor relented first. "Okay, pal. I will. But in return, you promise when that day comes, you'll be on your best behavior. None of this crap I've been listening to the last few minutes."

Andrew released his grip on the handle and allowed Taylor to open the door. Once the two were inside, Taylor secured Andrew in his storage compartment without any further exchange of words. He turned the android off and closed and locked the compartment door. Once out of the lab, he mulled over their conversation, wondering how much of it he needed to pass along to his boss. *I'm worried about him,* Taylor thought. *But for now, I'm going to put it out of my mind and enjoy an evening with Jaelyn.*

Chapter Five – Celebration

Taylor caught up with Brady and Ashlyn in the parking lot. Before they could jump into Brady's car, Taylor spotted Moira and Kazuhiro Sora leaving the building. "Wait a minute," he told the others, "I want to see if they might join us."

"The director of the Science Division? Are you kidding me?" Brady said. "She's ten salary grade levels above you. Why don't you invite the president, too? His company would make her feel right at home."

"Moira Lambert is not the stiff that your guy, Jerome Mosby, is," Taylor said. "She likes to associate with the people in her organization."

Taylor waved at the two. Moira paused and waved back with a beaming smile.

"We're going to the Interstellar Club to celebrate. We'd love to have you join us," Taylor shouted.

Moira checked her watch and then glanced at Kazuhiro. "We're meeting Crawford for dinner in an hour, but we have time to have a drink with the all-star crew of Ares I. We'll meet you there."

Taylor got into Brady's car. Once he closed the door, he ribbed Brady. "Let's see you try that with Mosby."

"No way, man. Just be on your best behavior, because it's your career that's at risk." Brady started the engine and drove to the club, a few blocks away. Once all were inside, Taylor and Ashlyn introduced Moira and Kazuhiro to Brady.

"Jaelyn is on her way," Taylor said. "We'll take that big table in the corner."

They ordered drinks. Before their order arrived, they were joined by Jaelyn.

"I'm happy to have an opportunity to chat with our twin mission specialists," Moira said. "Kazuhiro works you two so hard that I don't normally have a chance to get acquainted. Tell me the latest about your experiment."

Ashlyn and Jaelyn exchanged glances, a little nervous about discussing information in front of Brady that Kazuhiro might prefer not be shared with a member of another organization.

"I want to come to a better understanding of how the H-B equipment enhances the extrasensory abilities that you two exhibit," Moira said.

Before Moira could continue, Kazuhiro jumped in to save the twins from their concern about what to discuss in front of others and what to keep to themselves. He reminded Moira and Brady as to why Ashlyn and Jaelyn had been chosen as mission specialists for the H-B experiment in the first place. In addition to possessing the qualifications for being a crew member—pilot experience, excellent health, physical capability, and education—they tested among the ninety-ninth percentile of over a thousand applicant twin pairs for their extrasensory perception abilities.

"We learned in early experiments that our equipment generates a Higgs-Boson field of . . . uh, well for conversational purposes among friends, let's just go ahead and use the term, "God Particles," while the equipment is in operation. The field, similar to a magnetic flux field surrounding electronic equipment, consists of a plasma stream of particles. They interact with the billions of similar particles in our human bodies, including our minds. That interaction amplifies the natural mental ability of the person immersed in the field to perceive thoughts transmitted by other people with similar capabilities," he said. "Using the equipment, Ashlyn and Jaelyn correctly identify images telepathically transmitted by the other more than eighty percent of the time."

"Surreal," Brady said.

"No, not surreal. If you have no trouble with radio waves and wireless connections being able to send images and sounds from a transmitter to a receiver, why should you consider Higgs-Boson particles sending images from one brain to another anything extraordinary?"

Moira agreed. "That's why we've invested a great amount of funds to test the physical limits of that capability. We want to see how far Ashlyn and Jaelyn can communicate with each other, using only their mental processes."

Brady sat back in his seat, happy to see their drinks had arrived. His expertise was piloting, not mental telepathy.

Taylor passed the drinks around and raised his glass, proposing a toast. "Here's to the success of our simulation today," he said. "And best wishes to A.J. and J.J. for their contributions."

All drank to the toast. After a sip, Moira set her glass on the table. "A.J. and J.J.?" she asked.

Taylor chuckled. "My nicknames for our twins—Ashlyn Johnson and Jaelyn Johnson. What two more famous nicknames could there be in Houston?"

Kazuhiro Sora looked a little confused, but Moira made the connection. "A.J.—the two-fisted Texan race driver at the Indy 500, and J.J.—the defensive end for the Texans. You're right—in their time, there were none better. Gosh, more than twenty years ago. Has it really been that long?"

They chatted a few moments more before Moira stood to excuse herself. "Kazuhiro and I must leave or Crawford's going to send out a posse for us. Enjoyed our conversation. Bye all."

A few moments later, Brady left, too, telling Taylor that he and Ashlyn could ride back to NASA with Jaelyn in her car. Taylor ordered a second drink for himself and Ashlyn, but Jaelyn declined. "I'm driving," she said.

"Okay, you two," Taylor said. "I noticed each of you kept quiet and let Mr. Kazuhiro explain the functioning of the H-B device. I think you know more than he discussed."

Again the twins looked at each other and then Ashlyn spoke. "We didn't want to say anything in front of Brady because the information we gave him would go straight to the top of his organization. Our careless disregard for confidential material would be a negative reflection on Moira Lambert. But . . ."

Taylor took a big swallow of his drink. "What?" he asked.

". . . uh, there's been a breakthrough."

"What kind of a breakthrough, Ashlyn?"

Jaelyn jumped into the conversation. "You know that one of the mission objectives is to use the H-B device to scan some of the geological anomalies on the surface of Phobos and date them, hopefully to dispel the rumors and conjecture that Phobos is a hollow, artificial satellite created by extraterrestrials."

"I am aware of that effort," Taylor said. "I also know that there is some concern that the rumor might be true. The Russians have accused us of already having that knowledge and destroying their probes to keep it a secret. They think we're worried that the world couldn't handle proof that we're not alone in the universe, so we keep it a secret."

Jaelyn glanced at several of the tables near to them to be sure no one was within hearing distance. "The breakthrough involves a phenomenon that would make several countries, if they knew, employ every attempt possible to steal the knowledge and weaponize it."

"Go on."

"We found that when someone is operating the H-B device, they are immersed in its field of flux and their extrasensory perception is greatly enhanced."

"That's what Kazuhiro told us. The two of you can score better than 80 percent on sensing the diagrams—stars, squares, triangles, and circles—the other is viewing."

"That's what has been released to the public, but since you're going on the mission with us, we'll let you know what we've discovered."

Taylor had no idea where Jaelyn was heading, but he focused on her every word.

"The ESP diagrams are kid stuff. When I'm operating the equipment," Ashlyn said, "I can see what Jaelyn sees. I can hear what she hears. And I can feel what she feels."

Taylor leaned against the back of the booth. "You mean she becomes your avatar in a sense?"

"Exactly."

Taylor thought a moment, shocked by the revelation. "So are you telling me that when—hypothetically of course—Jaelyn and I have sex . . . uh . . . you, uh . . . are aware of it?"

Taylor winced when Jaelyn banged her knee against his under the table.

"Only if I'm operating the H-B device at the time, so be careful."

Jaelyn's face turned ever deepening shades of red. "Let's change the subject to a more realistic concern. If our enemies were to gain this knowledge and capability, they could develop it for intelligence purposes, making old-fashioned spying like child's play."

"Is Moira Lambert aware of this breakthrough?"

"Every bit of it. That's why the experiment is a major component of the mission. We want to test the absolute limits of its capability."

Taylor swallowed the rest of his drink and let out a nervous chuckle. "And to think—up until a few moments ago—my biggest concern was how much secret information Andrew might know. Now I have to worry about everything I whisper in Jaelyn's ear!"

Accompanied by the flight director, Jerome Mosby barged into the security office of the Johnson Space Center and glared at the on-duty captain of the guard. "Get me the security camera tape of the simulation lab for today," he said.

"Uh . . . I'll need to see your I.D. first," the captain said.

Mosby withdrew his wallet, flipped it open to his I.D. and shoved it under the nose of the captain. He nodded toward the flight director. "He's with me."

The captain had a "holy shit" moment when he recognized his visitor to be a senior director from NASA headquarters in D.C.

"Right away, sir," he said, scurrying toward a stack of DVDs. "I'll put it up on the center monitor screen. Where do you want me to start?"

"At about ten this morning," he answered. Then he looked at the flight director. "That's the time we finished the mission review. Wasn't it?"

The flight director nodded his confirmation. Both watched the screen as the tape began to play. As soon as they saw Taylor enter the lab, Mosby said, "Keep going but slow down."

They saw Taylor approach the storage cabinet for Andrew and reach for the lock. He paused a moment in thought and then opened the door. Taylor's body obstructed the view of the android.

"Damn," Mosby said. "That's when he must have turned the droid on and told him about the planned emergency simulation, but I can't confirm it from this angle."

Turning away from the monitor, Mosby asked the captain. "Have you got any other cameras that show a different angle?"

"Sorry, sir. I don't"

"Well, back this tape up again. I want to have another look."

The captain did as told, but in his nervousness overshot the starting point. He pressed the "play" button on the remote. A second, but blurred image could be seen at the cabinet door, working with the lock.

"Whoa!" Mosby said. "What's that? Replay it."

All three watched the tape several times, trying to identify the person, but the intruder wore a cap and stood facing away from the camera, trying not to be recognized.

Mosby glared at the flight director. "Now we've got two problems. The first is a breach of confidentiality by Taylor. I'll take care of that one when I meet with Lambert. But now we've got an intruder. I'm heading over to the chief of security. We've got to catch this guy. Could be anything—from theft to espionage and even sabotage. Could put the whole Ares program at risk."

Mosby and the flight director stormed out of the security office without saying a word to the captain.

After enjoying the last spoonful of a scrumptious ice cream desert at his favorite restaurant—The Eyes of Texas on the boardwalk at Kemah—Crawford asked the waiter if he and the two others in his party could move to a secluded room. "For a private conversation," he said.

The waiter assisted Moira with her chair and beckoned them to follow. He led them to a small lounge off the main dining room, complete with comfortable sofas, subdued lighting, and a cozy fireplace—even though it was July in Houston and 102 degrees outside—a fireplace was a prerequisite for Texan ambiance. Crawford slipped the waiter a large bill and whispered, "Thanks."

"No problem. This room's not in use until nine o'clock this evening when the combo arrives. You can have it to yourselves until then." The waiter took their after-dinner drink orders and scurried from the room, pulling the folding doors closed behind him.

At the front of the room stood a small, semi-circular stage, which contained a grand piano, a drum set, and a bass violin—instruments ready for the ensemble to play later. After helping Moira to her seat, Kazuhiro turned to Crawford and said, "I beg your indulgence, sir. If you don't mind, I have a surprise for your lady."

Crawford nodded his assent, slightly bewildered by the comment, but open to suggestion.

Kazuhiro walked to the stage, and, making a big production of flourishing imaginary coattails, sat at the piano. A transformation came over his face, and with a fluid, artistic motion, he reached for the keyboard with his hands. Before he began to play, he announced the piece: "Rachmaninoff's Prerude in C-sharp minor." He emphasized the word "Prerude" with a big grin, but quickly added, "Just kidding, Rambert!"

Kazuhiro leaned his head back, with his eyes closed, and began the strong, dominant introduction to the expressive, but difficult, concerto.

Moira listened, overwhelmed by his talent. She did not know he played the piano. She enjoyed seeing a side of him he seldom shared in public.

Kazuhiro worked through the concerto's intricate chords, its ever-changing dynamics, and its complex tempos. Just before the end, however, he introduced a jazz phrase into the melody line. A huge grin came over his face, and, bar by bar, he allowed the jazz rendition to overtake the classical score. He continued playing, now emphasizing his jazz interpretation of the music.

A man in a ponytail, wearing an ebony, long-sleeved, flowing dress shirt, poked his head through the doors and listened a moment. He stepped into the room, strode to the stage, and grabbed the neck of the bass and improvised a bass line to compliment the jazz melody. He nodded to another man, similarly dressed, at the door who took a position at the drum set and, using brushes, provided a sophisticated, upbeat tempo for the performance.

Moira smiled with delight and reached for Crawford's hand on the table. She squeezed it. Crawford could feel the rhythm coursing through her fingertips, a pulsing that increased with a crescendo into an expression of desire. Crawford was pleased he had gone along with Kazuhiro's suggestion.

All too soon, the music stopped. Kazuhiro rose and shook the hands of the two men who had joined him.

"We need a jazz pianist—ours is quitting," one said. "Interested?"

"I might be," Kazuhiro answered, "but I have a day job that takes priority."

The man offered his card. "Anytime you change your mind, give me a call."

The musicians, satisfied with the instrumental set up for their ensemble, left the room. Kazuhiro rejoined the others at their table.

"Kazuhiro, I've worked with you for more than ten years and never knew you had that in you. It was wonderful. Where did you learn to play like that?" Moira asked.

"My mom and dad emigrated from Japan and began new lives in America. Dad came over to teach physics at UCLA. Mom was a classical pianist and taught piano. As a boy, I would listen to her practice hour upon hour. When she finished, I would climb up on the piano bench and imitate her playing. I can't explain it, but the piano came easy for me. Before long I could play some of her difficult pieces by first listening to them and then repeating them, note for note."

"You're a musical prodigy," Moira said.

"I'm not sure that's the term I would use, because my first love was physics. All the natural laws and the order of things in the universe fascinated me. Dad encouraged me. I found music to represent a set of incredible natural laws that were as much a part of the universe as physics. Tones are, after all, merely frequencies—the same as radio waves, light beams, and even atomic particles. My mind hungers for it all, absorbs the science, and combines and rearranges things to make progress—whether it's a jazz rendition of Rachmaninoff or an experiment with a Higgs-Boson particle."

Moira sipped her drink. "Since you brought that subject up, I do know one thing about you from your past. I read that you built your own particle collider in your basement for a science fair project. You won the California fair, but you came in second at the national fair in Albuquerque. An unbelievable project for an eighth grader. Why did you not win the national?"

Now it was Kazuhiro's turn to laugh. "I built the collider with scavenged parts with the help of a grant from my school. I remember asking my mom if I could use our basement to build a 300-billion-electron-volt atom smasher for my project. She looked a little shocked but agreed."

"How big was it? Did it work?"

"It kind of looked like Frankenstein's waffle iron on steroids, with copper coiled, horseshoe magnets accelerating protons to collide with other protons, leaving traces of sub-atomic particles on film. But it worked—at least at home."

"What happened at Albuquerque?"

"When I turned it on, it blew all the fuses in the electrical supply circuits. The whole convention center went dark."

Moira stifled a laugh, but Crawford couldn't and chortled aloud, receiving an elbow in his side from Moira for his transgression. After a moment, both regained their composure.

"A shame," Moira said. "After all that work."

"No. It became a real triumph. One of the visitors was a member of the MIT board. After he saw my project and heard me explain how it worked, he made a few calls and offered me a scholarship in physics, telling me to 'keep my grades up' during high school. After getting my PhD from MIT, I received an offer to work with the team of physicists on the Hadron collider, in

Europe. That's how I got started with my work on the Higgs-Boson particle—better known as the 'God Particle.'"

"I graduated in the field of orbital mechanics from MIT fifteen years after you," Moira said. "You were a legend there. You still are."

"A regend, Rambert?" Kazuhiro said, once again joking. "No, I'm just a scientist with a home and family in L.A. trying to eke out a living working with NASA in Houston."

Moira raised her glass. "Here's a toast to my favorite legend. May you always enjoy life while you contribute to our understanding of the universe that surrounds us."

After honoring the toast by taking a sip from his glass, Kazuhiro became pensive. "My parents were Shinto—'way of the gods'—a Japanese religion that focuses on the connection between present-day Japan and its ancient past. They raised me as a Shintoist, but today I believe in all faiths. To me, life, the universe—and God, are all one. And the closer we get to a complete understanding of the sub-atomic particles, the closer we get to God."

A few minutes later, the room lights dimmed and the lights on the stage brightened. The band leader introduced himself and the other members and said they would begin the set with soft jazz renditions of popular songs and would take requests from the audience. "We love to improvise," the leader said. "Give us a challenge." A few moments after they began playing the first request, Moira excused herself to go to the women's room.

While she was away, Crawford took the opportunity to talk with Kazuhiro. He expressed his fascination with Kazuhiro's work and asked a number of questions about some of the details of the equipment design. Having had a few drinks and enjoying the relaxed atmosphere, Kazuhiro shared more information than would be normal for him but stopped short of providing anything critical.

Crawford shifted his attention to something more personal. "Kazuhiro," he said. "I've wondered about your name. Both your names are given—not family—names. With the Japanese convention of the given name being last in the order—opposite to ours—I'm never sure what to call you, Kazuhiro or Sora."

Kazuhiro chuckled. "Both my names are what you call first names. Kazuhiro means 'harmony' and Sora means 'sky.' Somewhere a long time ago, my ancestors misspelled our family name of Saro and used Sora instead. For some reason it stuck."

"What do you prefer to be called then?"

"Kazuhiro. But people call me both. No problem."

Crawford set his glass on the table and shook his head. "Too many syllables for a West Texas rancher. I think I'll call you 'Kaz' instead. Makes it a whole lot simpler."

Kazuhiro laughed. "That's fine if I can call you 'Tex,' since it's easier for me to pronounce than your real name."

Both men clinked their glasses together, enjoying the camaraderie.

Crawford jotted something down on his cocktail napkin, placed a five dollar bill in it and handed it to a member of the wait staff passing by. "Take it to the band leader," he said.

When Moira returned to the table the men stood to greet her. Kazuhiro bowed. Moira noticed the look of mischief on each of their faces. "You've both been up to something," she said.

Denying it, Crawford took her hand and asked her to dance with him. As they stepped to the floor, the ensemble began playing "The Lady in Red." Moira hugged Crawford. "You're such a romantic," she said. "Do you remember what we were doing the first time we listened to it?"

"I do," Crawford said. He brushed his fingertips against her red scarf, held her close and began dancing with her. The more the strains played on, the tighter she pressed her body against his. When the music stopped, she held on to him with a lingering embrace. She nibbled his ear and whispered, "Take me back to our room."

Chapter Six – Apart

The next morning in their hotel suite, Moira brought Crawford coffee in bed. "Morning, my love," she said.

"Morning, to you, too," Crawford replied, rubbing his eyes. "You kept me up late again last night."

"I couldn't get that jazz rendition of 'The Lady in Red' off my mind," Moira said. "There was only one thing I knew that would help."

"I should've recorded the performance while I had the chance," Crawford said, caressing her knee. "You never know when it might come in handy again."

Moira laughed and kissed him. "You've never needed music before!"

Crawford reached for her.

"Not now," she said. "Finish your coffee while I get dressed. You've got to run me to the airport."

Crawford took a couple of sips. "Damn, that's awful stuff. Must be the hotel's brand." Then he changed his tone. "You and I are always having to leave each other. We spend a lot of time apart."

"Makes the homecomings better."

"I know, but don't you ever get tired of it? I do. I get worried about you. You're in a high-stakes game." Crawford frowned, struggling for the right words. "This Ares mission. Well—God forbid—what if something terrible were to happen? How would you be able to handle that? It could destroy you."

Moira knew he had a point. Sometimes she had nightmares about any one of a number of horrible possibilities occurring. She didn't need to be reminded of some of NASA's previous catastrophic failures.

"Crawford, I do my job to the best of my ability. I can't guarantee bad things won't happen, but I'm confident that my efforts, combined with those of all the other good people I work with, will keep that possibility to an absolute minimum."

"But there's still a risk."

"Crawford, that's not fair. Risk is the price we pay for working at the boundary of scientific exploration, and—"

"And you've made your contribution. Why keep pressing? Let someone else step in."

"Why? I'll tell you why—I believe in what I'm doing, and I'm damn good at it. The exploration of our universe is a vital element in our quest for knowledge. We could choose instead to try and avoid risk by crawling back into caves and suffering the illnesses, injuries, and shortened life-expectancies of our ancestors."

Crawford sighed. "I know you're right. And I know the success of this mission could put you in line for the NASA Administrator's job when he retires, but—"

"There's that 'but' again. But what?"

"Wouldn't you like to retire and spend all your time with me on our ranch?"

"Someday, I'd like to do nothing better. But as long as we're being honest with each other, I worry more about you in *your* work."

"Oh, yeah," Crawford answered. "All I've got to deal with are rattlesnakes, rustlers, and bucking broncos."

"That's *not* the line of work I meant."

"I *know* what you meant, but we can't talk about that."

Moira responded with a stony silence. After a moment, she said, "Fine."

Her intensity caught Crawford off guard, but she changed the subject.

"Hurry and get dressed," she said. "We've got to go."

They suffered through a tense ride to the airport with neither speaking to the other. When Crawford pulled to a stop in front of the small terminal, Moira turned toward him, and he saw a tear running down her cheek.

"I'm sorry," she said. "I always miss you when we're apart, and I can't wait to see you again."

He embraced her and held her until she settled down.

"When does *your* flight leave?" she asked.

"I'm staying over a few days. I'm meeting with representatives of a Chinese company that want to sell me on a project to build a wind farm atop one of the mesas on our ranch. There could be a lot of money in it, but I'm not yet sold on the economic or environmental benefits of their project. But we'll see."

The co-pilot approached their car and interrupted by asking Moira if he could help with her luggage. "The engines are spooling up, ma'am. We need to get on board."

Moira brushed Crawford's cheek with a kiss and rushed to the entrance without looking back.

The next morning, Moira arrived at the NASA headquarters building in D.C.—late again due to heavy traffic, but unconcerned because she knew she had no meetings on her schedule until mid-afternoon. Inserting her key to allow the elevator to take her to the secure suite on the top floor, she gave some thought as to how she would spend her free morning. *Maybe I should call Crawford,* she thought. *I know he can't talk about his work. I shouldn't have*

pressed him. Deciding to give them both a bit more time before calling, she stepped from the elevator when the doors opened and strode toward her office, adjacent to that of the administrator.

She had not finished booting up her computer when her phone rang.

"Yes?" she answered.

"The administrator wants to see you right away," her aide said. "He has a visitor in his office. Says it's urgent."

"Thanks." Moira walked to the administrator's door, straightening her scarf as she approached. Once there, she tapped and entered the office when asked. She saw Administrator Durand seated at a small couch in front of his desk. In a chair facing him, a stranger sat, erect and in a posture of attention—a tall, black man in his late forties, dressed in a conservative, charcoal-gray suit and wearing a solid navy-blue tie. Both men stood to greet Moira.

"Morning, Moira," Administrator Durand said. "I want to introduce Agent Emmett Nelson, the head of the Counter Terrorism Division of the National Security Branch of the FBI." Durand continued. "Agent Nelson, this is my Senior Director of the Science Division, Moira Lambert."

Moira took a few steps forward with an outstretched hand to greet him, but Nelson reached for his wallet and opened it to show his badge and ID, leaving Moira in an awkward stance. She withdrew her hand and let it fall to her side.

"Morning," Nelson said.

Before she could reply, Administrator Durand began to explain. "Agent Nelson has briefed me on a situation that you must be made aware of," the administrator said. "I'll let him tell you what he has told me. Please, let's all sit."

The agent got straight to the point. "Ms. Lambert, we have credible evidence that operatives from a foreign country are attempting to sabotage the Ares program."

Moira sat back in disbelief, stunned by the revelation. *As if normal risks weren't enough of a hazard,* she thought. *Now we've got to worry about . . .*

"Terrorists?" she asked.

"We can't be certain, yet. That's why we need your help."

Moira's expression remained unchanged, but her mind reeled. *I don't need this,* she thought. *Not after my discussion yesterday with Crawford about risks.* Her professionalism prevailed. "What can I do?" she asked.

The agent briefed her on the information they had—about the security camera showing an intruder plus some other breeches of security. "The CIA has been tailing a couple of suspicious persons, one a U.S. citizen and two others here on visas. We think one or more of them may contact you."

"Why?"

"To get information about the Ares program."

"They won't get it from me."

The agent shrugged. "We know, but here comes the difficult part."

Moira anticipated where he might be headed, but his request still shocked her when she heard him say it aloud. "We want you to give them whatever they ask."

Moira shook her head. "No! I won't. I can't risk the safety of the mission."

The agent and the administrator exchanged glances. Moira took a few deep breaths.

The agent continued. "It may be something simple, like an entry code, or something technical, like the amount of fuel on board. But whatever it is they want, give it to them without any deviations from fact.

"I don't understand why I should do that."

The agent explained it was the only way they could develop leads on the effort to sabotage the mission and to intercede."

"If you don't help us, the mission could experience a disaster," he said. "We will be monitoring all your communications—phone, computer—everything. You'll be under constant surveillance. It's the only way we can get a handle on this effort."

Agent Nelson handed Moira his card. "If someone contacts you, or even if you notice some suspicious or unusual behavior of someone within your group, call me. I can always be reached. Give me a detailed description of the contact as soon as possible after it happens."

Moira studied the card and glanced at the administrator. He nodded his head.

"Okay. If it will reduce the risk for the mission," she said.

"And one other thing," Agent Nelson said. "The three of us are the only ones to have this information. No one else—family, including spouses—is to know."

The cab screeched to a halt in front of Houston's convention center. Crawford paid the fare, tipped the cabbie, and stepped from the air-conditioned cab into the brutal summer heat. Crossing the landscaped entrance plaza complete with its series of computer-controlled, water jet fountains, he swore under his breath at the oppressive humidity. Crawford rushed past the marquee advertising the "International Trade Show for Sustainable Energy" and entered the center, thankful for the coolness of its interior. Inside, a bustling crowd of visitors milled around exhibits, snacking on popcorn, hotdogs, and sodas.

Crawford hurried down an aisle lined with exhibition booths, avoiding hawkers and representatives trying to hand him literature about their products. Reaching an exhibit for wind turbines, he introduced himself to one of the attendants and asked for the man with whom he had an appointment. "Mr. Hsu, please," he said. "I'm Crawford Lambert."

The attendant whispered, "Mezzanine level. Suite 102," nodding toward the elevator.

Once outside the door to the suite, Crawford adjusted the brim of his hat, and knocked. A moment passed. Then the door opened. A slim man wearing a tailored suit invited him in. The man had a petite face with black hair neatly combed back. He shook Crawford's hand. "Come in, Mr. Lambert. I've been expecting you." The man spoke perfect English, except for an occasional hint of a Chinese accent. "Would you care for some tea?"

"No, thank you," Crawford said. "Let's get on with business. I've been working with you for months. It's time to close the deal."

The man motioned for Crawford to take a seat. He opened a briefcase and withdrew a sheaf of papers. "My client is prepared to offer you a 400 megawatt wind farm, constructed with our most sophisticated, energy-efficient wind turbines at no cost to you. My client would provide you ten percent of the earnings from the project for life."

The man paused to let his comments sink in.

He continued. "In return, you would agree to provide my client with, uh . . . let's just say, uh . . . critical information that he might need to maintain successful operation of the project."

Crawford removed his hat and set it on his knee.

"Do you understand the terms of the contract?" the man asked.

"I do."

"Then I needn't remind you that the details of the contract are, uh . . . sensitive. Any disclosure would be cause for termination."

Crawford smiled. "You're referring to terminating the *contract*, of course."

"Of course—I'm sure you understand what I mean."

The man reached into his vest pocket and withdrew a fountain pen. "For legal purposes I'll need you to sign this document. It references the project and your rights to ten percent of the earnings."

"Nothing else?" Crawford asked.

"Of course not."

Crawford took the pen and with a flourish, signed the paper. He got up from his chair and placed his hat on his head, ready to leave. Before he reached the door, the man said, "We'll be contacting you soon. As always, the contact will be discreet."

Working at her desk, Moira looked up in surprise when Jerome Mosby nonchalantly walked into her office without knocking. The working relationship between the two had always been strained because they didn't particularly like each other. Adding to the stress, each knew they were both on the short list for promotion to NASA Administrator Durand's position when he retired. But Mosby had never rudely ignored basic office protocols before.

"We need to talk," he said.

Moira tabbed her iPad's calendar and shook her head. "I don't see that we had an appointment today."

"This won't take long." Without being offered, Mosby sprawled in one of the chairs facing her desk. "You've got a problem in your organization. Besides tolerating a robot that's confused about his role and running a rabbit hutch—"

"A *rabbit hutch*? You can do better than that. That's a term from the middle of the last century."

Ignoring her comment, Mosby continued. "Yes, besides running a rabbit hutch for crew members overdosed on hormones and doing eighth grade science project experiments, your security is lousy."

Moira listened with a noncommittal expression. "Go on," she said.

"Security videos show that someone—possibly a mole in your own group—tried to break in to your android's storage compartment. There's no telling what they might have been up to, but the possibilities are alarming."

"Do you have any details other than what you've discussed?"

"No."

"Have you had your say then?"

"I've said enough."

Moira rose from her chair and walked around her desk. She rested against its front edge and leaned forward toward Mosby. "Then hear me and listen well. We're dealing with human lives and the prestige of the U.S. space program—not to mention the billions of dollars in funds for the effort. If you think that I or anyone else in my organization would put those lives and that prestige at risk, then the next time you better come with facts to substantiate your charges. I am fully capable of handling any breach of security myself. You have enough to do to run your own organization without making accusations about mine."

Moira grabbed a sheaf of papers from her desk and buzzed her aide. He waited at the door not wishing to interrupt. "Come on in. Mr. Mosby and I have finished our discussion, and he is leaving," she said. "Please take these documents and see that they are properly filed."

Chapter Seven - The Ranch

The days drifted into late October, temperatures finally cooling—even in Texas. Each fall, Moira and Crawford hosted the leadership of her division at the Lambert ranch for a week-long conference to evaluate division personnel, review the accomplishments of the current year versus objectives, and develop strategies and goals for the forthcoming year.

Crawford always attempted to provide Moira's guests with an unforgettable experience, from tours of their ranch, to staying in rustic accommodations in a stone building with a corrugated tin roof, and to a chuck wagon barbecue complete with a country western band. Crawford led horseback rides for the adventurous to the tops of mesas to gaze at the spectacular sunset, followed by an evening of stargazing around a campfire. For those less inclined, Crawford on other nights would lead a convoy of ATV's in his unique, cherry red golf cart equipped with a mini-refrigerator filled with goodies and, of course, a variety of local beers.

The destination would be the rippling waters of a scenic creek bed for an evening of story telling and camaraderie. The guests loved the leadership meeting and many were able to bring their spouses to share in the fun.

During the day, however, Moira ran the various sessions with a tight agenda, exhibiting a mixture of a tough disciplinarian and a helpful ally. None of the other three senior directors enjoyed the rapport with their organizations as did she. As at home on horseback as behind a desk, she knew of no better place to work and relax than at their ranch.

One evening around a campfire, Kazuhiro Sora—feeling mellow after a few sudsy beers—dared ask her a question.

"Ms. Lambert, I've known you for a long time. We've been through a lot together. I'd like to ask you a personal question—one I've wondered about for many years. Do you mind?"

The others around the glowing fire overheard the question and became silent, wondering what the question would be.

"As long as I can answer it in front of Crawford, I don't mind at all," Moira said, leaning against her husband.

Kazuhiro hesitated at first, a little concerned he might have overstepped the bounds of courtesy. He cleared his throat and then asked, "You always wear a touch of red—sometimes subtle but other times bold. And—"

"You wonder why I do."

"Yes, if I may."

Moira touched her bright red neckerchief and smiled. She became pensive.

"Red was my mother's favorite color. After my dad passed away at an early age, she sacrificed a great deal to see that I had the opportunities she never had—including an education. She encouraged me to excel in my endeavors, always telling me that I could do anything I set about to do. She reminded me that she chose my name, Moira, because it meant 'destiny,' and she believed I could have a great future. My mentor and, uh . . . my ideal, I miss her terribly. She never had the opportunity to meet my love, Crawford, or see me advance in NASA."

Moira paused, overcome with emotion. Then with a smile, she said, "I always wear red for her memory."

Kazuhiro didn't know how best to respond and remained quiet, searching for words.

Crawford put his arm around Moira and drew her close to him. "She also loves to wear boots in my honor," he said, breaking the somber mood with humor. Moira laughed, as did the others.

"As long as we're talking about personal stuff," Crawford said, "Kaz, you like to wear boots, too—and Stetsons. How would you like to have a real cowboy experience?"

Kazuhiro didn't know how to respond to the question, worried that it might be a setup for a prank. "Maybe, Crawford. It depends."

"Why don't you join me on a trail ride to next year's Houston Livestock Show and Rodeo?"

"Trail ride?"

"In the days before the rodeo starts, trail riders converge upon Houston from towns all across the region, some spending as long as ten days on the road. I always ride my favorite group from Victoria, Texas, and Moira always joins me the last day of the ride. It's authentic. We go on horseback in all kinds of weather, sleeping in bedrolls, and eating grub from a chuck wagon. We'd be happy to have you."

Kazuhiro's expression morphed into that of a person realizing a dream had come true. "I'd love it. When does the trail ride start?"

"Next year in late February, a couple of weeks before your astronauts blast off for the International Space Station."

Kazuhiro looked at Moira, studying her face for any sign of disapproval. "If my schedule permits, I would like to join you. But you know, my job is first priority," he said.

"No problem. I face that issue with Moira every year. If things work out, we'll plan on it."

The fire had died down to glowing embers. Moira stood and suggested they head back to the ranch house. "Important day tomorrow. Everyone better get a good night's sleep."

The next morning, Moira and her leadership team worked through a series of budgetary issues, finishing with a list of reduction contingencies in case budgets got cut. At noon, Crawford entered the meeting room, accompanied by a couple of his ranch hands carrying serving pans filled with berries and other fruit for those who worried about healthy diets to fried chicken, roast beef, and French fries for those who did not. Canisters of tea and lemonade, cans of soda, and bottles of water were placed next to the food. Apple pie and peach cobbler were set out for dessert, next to a tub of vanilla ice cream.

Once the serving table had been set, Crawford dismissed his hands and rang a wrought-iron dinner bell. The guests needed no second invitation and soon their plates were piled with food while chatter filled the room.

Crawford noticed on the agenda that Kazuhiro Sora would be giving an overview of his Higgs-Boson experiment after lunch. Once lunch had been finished and bathroom breaks taken, the group came back to order. Moira introduced the Higgs-Boson topic, pointing out it would be an overview of the subject for those who had no direct responsibility for it.

"It's a fascinating, scientific effort that will allow us to determine how long the geological anomalies on Phobos have existed. Once we analyze the data, we'll be able to tell whether the pyramid on the surface is a natural formation or whether it is an artifact left by—uh, for our purposes today, let's just say—others."

During her introduction, Crawford busied himself stacking pans, dishes, and utensils on trays. Once finished, he tiptoed to the door and motioned for his helpers to remove all the items from the room. After his hands had completed their work, Crawford remained behind, a pitcher of tea in one hand and lemonade in the other, filling the glasses of the participants as Kazuhiro Sora began his presentation.

Kazuhiro explained in layman terms how the Higgs-Boson equipment, using the field generated by the "God Particle," could photograph an object and present a complex array on a monitor. The equipment could then portray that same object at various stages of time. When the array changed, it meant the object was no longer present. "We can by analysis determine when the object first came into being," Kazuhiro said. "We will be able to tell if the small pyramid in question was of the same age as the other surface characteristics or if it came at a later time. In that case, it could mean that it was built by, uh . . . others, as Ms. Lambert suggested."

Moira stepped in. "One of the overriding objectives of the first Ares mission is to determine whether or not Phobos is a natural satellite—a captured asteroid—or if it's artificial, an unlikely, but earth-shattering outcome. We have briefed the president on this remote possibility, and he is developing a strategy as to how to deal with that event should it become necessary."

"What about the work with the set of twins?" one of the participants asked. "We've heard they can read each other's minds."

During the question, Moira noticed Crawford still serving beverages in the room. Before responding to the question, she frowned at him and with a quick flick of her eyes toward the door, let him know he should leave. Crawford recognized the subtle signal and without hesitation, set the pitchers down and departed.

Moira began her answer, not missing a beat. "As monumental as the possible finding would be that Phobos was an artificial satellite, the ability of the Higgs-Boson experiment to allow communication between minds is even more dramatic," Moira said. "And it is a capability that will be sought by nations other than the U.S. for ulterior purposes. Any details of the Higgs-Boson equipment or its operation must be kept closely guarded. We lost our nuclear edge through espionage. We cannot afford a similar outcome with this equipment, so be forewarned—what you hear today is extremely sensitive."

Late that evening, after the guests had returned to their rooms, Moira sat next to Crawford, shoes off and curled up against him on the couch in their den. Sipping nightcaps, they both took pleasure in watching the flickering glow from the crackling flame inside the stone fireplace. They seldom had the opportunity to enjoy being alone together, but Moira broke the spell by criticizing Crawford's indiscretion earlier that day.

"You can't do that."

"What?"

"Intrude on our meeting."

"Gosh, dear. It was an oversight. I'm sorry."

"I know you meant nothing by it. And I also know you are cleared to hear any information we might cover—but my staff members aren't aware of that. I got some questioning looks from a few of them about your presence."

Crawford swallowed the last of his drink and set the empty glass on the coffee table.

"Another?" Moira asked.

"No, thanks. It's time for bed. Breakfast is before sunrise tomorrow morning, and then we have to get your guests to the airport and you on your way to D.C."

Moira finished her drink and gathered up both glasses. She stood, but before she could start for the kitchen, Crawford grabbed her and gave her an endearing hug. "Are we okay?" he asked.

"We are, but don't you go interrupting my meetings again. I don't need to give anyone reason to question my integrity. There's enough crap going on without adding to the stack."

"I won't. I promise."

Crawford checked his watch. "You know, it's really not that late," he said, patting her rear.

Moira shook her head, but grinned. "Oh, I think it is."

"We'll see."

Chapter Eight – Awakening

Strapped inside his storage compartment, Andrew fluttered his eyelids and then opened his eyes wide. At first he stared straight ahead, but after a brief moment, he looked from side to side. He could see nothing in the pitch-black interior of his cabinet. Awaiting the booting up process to complete his activation, Andrew allowed himself to think. *No more reliance on humans to wake me up. No more death experiences.*

During his most recent simulator session, Andrew had managed to insert a shunt in his computer circuitry that allowed him to be placed in hibernation but enabled himself to self-activate when he desired. He had spent several prior sessions secretly fabricating the shunt in the lab. *Good thing that Taylor spends so much time on the phone talking to Jaelyn. Never could have done it otherwise.*

Once his control circuitry adjusted the light-sensitivity of his eyes to that of night vision goggles, Andrew freed his right arm from its latch and reached for the door release. *Careful about the security camera,* he reminded himself. The interior door release required no code to operate. Instead, a simple button had been added in the aftermath of an OSHA inspection to prevent potential entrapment of some overly inquisitive child. Once installed, the interior button had been the butt of numerous inside jokes as to the lack of OSHA's common sense.

The joke's on them, Andrew thought as he pressed the release button. The door sprang ajar. Now secure in his ability to control his own destiny, Andrew pulled the door shut and went back into hibernation.

Chapter Nine – Escape

Jaelyn spent a late night at the lab in an office cubicle keying into the computer answers to the questions from her twin sister that popped up in her mind.

Your favorite color?

"Blue," she typed.

Number?

"Twenty-seven."

Name of a face card and suit?

"King of Hearts."

The computer screen in front of her gave her a few seconds to provide each answer. The longer she worked, the more difficulty she had deciding upon her response. *Will this session ever end?* She wondered, her mind growing weary from concentrating so hard. During a pause in the mental questions, Jaelyn laid her head in her arms. In a few moments she drifted off to sleep.

A gentle rap at the door interrupted Ashlyn's thought processes. *Thank God for a break.* She stepped to the door and opened it, surprised to see Taylor standing there. She beckoned him to enter and turned back toward her desk.

Taylor reached around her from behind and pulled her back into his body, kissing the nape of her neck and pressing himself against her. Passion flared up inside her, and she turned to face him, embracing him in return. She pulled his shirt above his waist and reached for his belt buckle in an awkward attempt to unfasten it. Taylor's hands were all over her, raising her level of excitement to a burning desire. How she had longed for him. Now it would happen.

She heard an inner voice, weak at first and then building in insistence.

Wait, she thought. *Stop! I can't go on with this. I can't betray Jaelyn.* But Taylor pressed her against the wall and began stripping her clothes.

"NO!" she screamed aloud. She placed the palm of her hand against his face and shoved as hard as she could. "STOP!"

Taylor's face at first shimmered and then wavered like an image reflected from the surface of a pond. The pressure of his body diminished. Without warning, Taylor disappeared, leaving Ashlyn staring at Kazuhiro Sora, wearing his lab coat, a perplexed expression on his face. Each blinked at the other for a moment of awkward silence. Out of breath, Ashlyn gasped, coming to terms with where she was and what had happened.

"You okay?" Kazuhiro asked.

"Where's my sister?"

"She's down the hall answering your telepathic questions." Kazuhiro answered, gesturing toward a large HD monitor. "Her replies are on the screen. But she stopped a few minutes ago."

Ashlyn became aware of what had happened, but looked to Kazuhiro for his verification.

"We were using the Higgs-Boson field to amplify my telepathic capabilities, weren't we?"

"Of course. We were running another test. You were doing quite well. Don't you remember?"

"I do—up until—"

"Did something happen?"

"I need to go check on my sister." Ashlyn said, and ran down the hall toward the room her sister was in. She knocked. Hearing no answer, she knocked again, this time louder. She shouted, "Jaelyn. Open the damn door."

"Give me a minute," Jaelyn said.

Ashlyn heard some muffled bustling from within before the door opened. Jaelyn appeared in the opening, her shirt rumpled and not completely tucked into her waist.

"Is Taylor with you?" Ashlyn asked.

Taylor emerged from behind the door, stuffing his shirttails in and sheepishly trying to look nonchalant.

"He, uh . . . he interrupted my session. He didn't know I was working with you." Jaelyn saw the look on her sister's face and made the connection. "Uh-oh. It happened, didn't it?"

"You're damn right it did. Come on back to Kazuhiro with me. We've got to set some ground rules."

The two women walked back down the hall to discuss the incident with Kazuhiro. Taylor followed at a distance, not sure whether he should or not.

Still shaken, Ashlyn explained to Kazuhiro in general terms what had happened. "When Jaelyn nodded off, her mind lost all resistance. I became Jaelyn, seeing and feeling the things she experienced."

Kazuhiro listened intently, then asked, "What should we do?"

Ashlyn and her sister exchanged glances. Taylor hung back, trying not to be drawn into the conversation. "We need an escape button," Ashlyn said. "We need a way to bail out of the experiment in case of some problem."

Kazuhiro Sora at first didn't think something that drastic was necessary. He said some rules could be put in place to avoid similar situations.

Ashlyn did not accept his solution. "This time, it was just embarrassing. But next time . . . well, I wouldn't wish anything bad on anybody, but what if Jaelyn were to have a nightmare—or worse . . . maybe a hallucination or even a seizure. I wouldn't want to get caught up in that, nor would she if the situation were reversed."

Jaelyn nodded, adding her support.

"It'd be tricky," Kazuhiro said. "You'd have to break out of the situation before you were trapped within it."

"Without an escape capability, the whole mission could be put at risk. What if Jaelyn were to be assaulted during one of our experiments and try to fight off her attacker in self defense? Would you like me to karate chop one of the other crew members thinking they were attacking me?"

Kazuhiro rubbed his chin, but remained silent. Then, folding his notes, he answered. "You have a good point. I'll work on something."

"You'd better," Ashlyn said. Reaching for Jaelyn, she said, "Come on, sis, we're going home."

The two of them walked down the hall, leaving Taylor standing with his mouth agape.

"What about me?" he asked.

"Take a shower," Ashlyn said.

After the women left, Taylor decided not to go home nor to take a shower. Instead he went to the simulator building, showed his ID to the night security guard and headed toward Andrew's storage compartment. Tapping in the code, Taylor opened the door and smiled when he saw Andrew asleep. Taylor inserted the multi-pronged pin of the thumb drive on his key chain and brought Andrew to life.

"Hi, pal," Taylor said when the droid opened his eyes.

"It must be late. We don't have anything scheduled," Andrew said. "What's up?"

Taylor unlatched the arm and leg restraints and let his friend out of storage. "Nothing. Just need to talk," he said. Taylor recounted the events from earlier that evening. When he finished, Andrew tried to minimize Taylor's concern.

"Nothing to worry about," he said. "You were an innocent bystander that got caught up in a touchy situation."

Taylor didn't buy it. "That's what I thought at first. *Nothing to it*, I told myself."

"What's the problem, then?"

I can't believe I'm sitting here talking to a robot, Taylor thought. *Not about this subject, anyway.*

Andrew raised his eyebrows, waiting for an answer.

"The problem is, uh . . . well, after I started to make a move on Jaelyn, I realized it wasn't her—it was Ashlyn instead."

"How?"

I'm talking to a robot with the brain of an Einstein, but the physical development of a pre-pubescent, fourteen-year-old boy.

"Andrew, when you've been with a woman, you can sense her every response. You can tell who she is, what she wants, and how ready she is. I could tell it wasn't Jaelyn. I knew it had to be Ashlyn."

"What's so wrong about that?"

"I *wanted* it to be Ashlyn. I wanted her. It's hard to put into words, but when you have a relationship with a twin, you, uh . . . you, well, some men in that situation—not me, of course— fantasize about what it'd be like to have sex with the other twin."

"I think I understand, but I'm not sure. After all, I'm not anatomically complete in that area."

Taylor sighed and shook his head. *I'm confiding in an inexperienced boy*, he thought.

But Andrew continued. "But, just so you know, you're not alone. Sometimes I too have . . . uh . . . *urges*."

"Urges? What do you mean by that comment?"

Andrew explained that the software algorithms that made him a competent commander, able to take decisive action when necessary, even under extreme pressure, also at times gave him manly "urges."

"That's why I'd like to go party with you and the other crew members. I know how to pilot a command module, but I want to know what it's like to be with a woman."

Both remained silent, thinking about the other's dilemma. Taylor broke the silence. "Sorry, pal. In your case, it's not going to happen. Maybe for future generations of droids, but not you—not with the present state of the art."

"Remember, I'm ageless," Andrew said. "I can always get an upgrade—when one becomes available. Until then, just let me go party with you and the others one time. You know—to satisfy some urges."

"We can't do that. I've explained that before. Too big a risk." Taylor said. "Now let's go back in the box."

Andrew's expression turned into one of dejection. "But we were having such a good talk. You know—the way men talk—man to man."

Taylor couldn't escape the irony of the phrase, but he didn't correct the droid. "In you go, pal. We'll talk some more at another time—man to man."

Crawford finished his job of greasing the gears on the antique Aermotor Windmill's water pump that fed the horse trough next to the ranch house. The vanes on the windmill were bright red, white, and blue wooden slats wired together in the form of a large, expanded peach basket. Three stories above the ground, Crawford, perched on a small platform surrounding the gear assembly, rose to his full height and gazed across the plains. A slight breeze foretold of December's coming brisk temperatures. The view never got old for Crawford. Overlooking his ranch, he could see the mesa where the wind farm project would be constructed if approved and, with the excellent visibility afforded by the clear sky, he saw the shadowy outlines of Amarillo's downtown buildings.

A rancher's dream, he thought. Then, remembering the lateness of the afternoon, he began the climb down the ladder from the top of the windmill to his golf cart parked below. *Mail should be here by now.* Once in the cart, Crawford sank into its plush, leather seat and raced down the mile-long drive to the ranch's entrance gate. He frowned at the coating of dust covering the cart's cherry-red, metallic paint, covered with enough layers of clear coat to give an illusion of depth. *Need to wash it before trucking it in a few weeks to Victoria for the trail ride.*

Though Crawford loved his horses, the cart was his pride and joy. Equipped with a walnut grained refrigerator and matching cabinetry, it had a top of the line stereo system and even an air conditioner and heating unit for use during temperature extremes.

The electric engine, chosen for its smooth drive and quiet operation, provided enough power for the cart to reach speeds nearing forty miles per hour. Speed and comfort were desirable benefits for a vehicle that provided personal transportation on a ranch that had been in Crawford's family for more than half a century and covered more than fifty thousand acres.

Leaving a rooster tail of dust behind him, Crawford made the trip to the front gate in a couple of minutes. He opened the mail box and reached into it, withdrawing a handful of envelopes and a small package, unmarked in a plain, brown wrapper. Puzzled, Crawford heard the screech of tires from a white car as it accelerated from a parked position a quarter mile away and raced out of sight.

Crawford waited a moment and then tossed the mail into the passenger seat. He withheld the package, shaking it and listening to its contents, trying to determine what might be inside. *One way to find out,* he thought. He ripped the paper away and saw a small box, previously used for jewelry. Holding the box at eye level, he raised the lid to peek inside for a preview. He could determine nothing. Exasperated, he removed the lid and tossed it aside. Lying in a bed of cotton and wrapped in a bag of clear plastic was an object accompanied by a note. He tore away the plastic and saw it held a thumb drive, but a unique one with a twenty-seven pin connector instead of the usual USB connection. Turning the object over and over, he inspected it but could find no clue as to its purpose.

He read the note. "Damn!" he swore aloud. He brushed his forehead with the palm of his hand and pushed back the brim of his hat. He reached into his pocket and withdrew his cell phone. Speed dialing his wife's direct line, he was relieved when she answered.

"Hi, love," Moira said, "You caught me about ready to head back to my apartment for the evening. What's up?"

"Just wanted to let you know, hon, that I'm returning to Houston for a few days."

"Anything wrong?"

"No. There's some more negotiation needed for the Chinese project. It's always something."

"Want me to join you?"

"Always, but save your time for the rodeo. That'll be a lot more exciting."

"Okay."

"I'll keep you posted. Bye."

"Bye, love."

Moira hung up her phone with a look of consternation on her face. *Something's up*, she thought. *A sudden trip to Houston? It's not like Crawford to be impulsive like that. The man plans everything down to the minutest detail. And normally he'd jump at the chance for us to be together—doesn't he want me to be there?*

Chapter Ten – Chief Astronaut

Like the commander of a U.S. Naval fleet, Chief Astronaut Isaiah Wilson, the International Space Station master had enormous responsibilities. Beginning a military career as a carrier fighter pilot in Iraq, Isaiah served for three tours over hostile territory, including his final one battling ISIS elements near the Turkish border. After completing his service, he qualified as an astronaut and made several trips to the International Space Station on the Russian Soyuz workhorse rocket.

During that time, the U.S. worked to develop the replacement vehicle for the defunct shuttle, the two-stage rocket, Eagle 1C, an unmanned cargo vehicle designed by a private firm, Apogee Systems, Inc., for the purpose of transporting supplies into low Earth orbit. After a series of successful launches, the company, under a contract with NASA, developed a manned version of the vehicle, named Eagle 2M. Isaiah served as copilot of the first manned flight of the upgraded vehicle. He made four trips to the station, the last three as the command pilot and accumulated a total of fourteen months aboard the station.

During its more than thirty years in orbit, the International Space Station had grown from a basic, manned satellite to a miniature city, complete with a series of docking ports that offered a multitude of nations and space vehicles the capability of unloading cargo and crew.

As the station grew in both size and population, at times hosting more than fifty residents, NASA recommended to the six member nations that a full time commander be given the responsibility to oversee station operations, proposing the position be rotated to a different member country every three years.

Chosen from a field of top astronauts, Isaiah became the first station commander with the title, Chief Astronaut. His skills, discipline, and capabilities proved to be so exceptional that upon completion of his first term, NASA asked him to serve a second term. At first, he held out, requesting that he be given opportunities to revisit Earth several times a year. NASA and the other countries agreed to his demands.

From the two-story bridge rising above the hub of the station, Isaiah could view every component of the facility. Live feeds of interior views and activities were shown on a series of HD monitor screens. Isaiah's personal quarters were located in the bridge so that he could be alerted by alarm if any situation of an emergency nature required his immediate attention—even during his time off.

Isaiah scanned all the sections of the station, on alert for any indication of a potential problem. The largest structure in his field of view was the assembly facility in which components of complex satellites could be put together and tested without requiring the workers to perform space walks. The sight of the assembly structure caused him to reflect back to his youth and his view of warehouse roofs from the fourth-floor bedroom he shared with his brother in Houston's Fifth Ward. He was grateful for his mother's parenting and her insistence that he work hard and become educated to make something of himself. *A long way for a black man from the ghetto*, he thought.

He never knew his dad who had abandoned his family shortly after his birth. He lost his brother to a stray bullet from a drug deal altercation and his mom passed away shortly after he entered military service. Isaiah thought of his brother every day and continually pushed himself to be worthy of his mother's sacrifices. Isaiah had no family remaining and had never married, but he did have a warm relationship with one of the female doctors in the medical center, Kayla Brewer. Their closeness and his lack of family on Earth made it easier for Isaiah to stay at the station for long periods of time. *My city*, he thought. Isaiah's fellow astronauts and station associates held him in the highest regard, often referring to him as "Mayor Isaiah" rather than using his formal title.

Isaiah shifted his gaze toward the other side of the station, shielding his eyes from the glare of the rising sun. During a brief time in each orbit when the sun first bathed the station with light and the Earth remained in darkness, the brilliant white of the station shined in contrast to the blackness of deep space and the Earth below. The Ares I vehicle assembly had been completed, and it stood docked at the station's largest port. All utilities—electrical power, oxygen, water, and others—had been fully activated so that technicians could perform functional tests of all the systems, a process that had been just begun and was on schedule to be completed before the astronauts arrived. The liquid fuel for the module's rockets would not be loaded until the day before launch.

For the previous year, subassemblies of the Ares I module had been brought to the station by a heavy-lift, low Earth orbit vehicle, Eagle 3HL, the third vehicle developed under contract. The heavy-lift vehicle was a much larger version of the original two-stage, unmanned vehicle that brought supplies to the station. The Eagle fleet of rockets proved to be extremely reliable and became the mainstay of the U.S. low Earth orbit fleet. All three vehicles would see extensive use during the Ares program.

In less than a month, the four Ares I crew members would be transported to the station in two flights because the Eagle 2M rocket had a capacity for only two at a time. Brady would pilot the first trip with Ashlyn as a passenger. Andrew would pilot the second a month later along with his passenger, Taylor. While awaiting the arrival of the second flight, Brady would assist the technicians in completing the readiness checks.

The Ares I module had four major sections. The first was the command module, consisting of the cockpit and the Higgs-Boson equipment. The nose cone of the command module contained the Photon Sail, a one-mile diameter web of electronic circuitry so fine that the whole sail could be compressed into a volume less than that of a hot tub. Behind the command module were the crew quarters that provided sleeping, kitchen, and bath facilities for the crew during the long trip. In the quarters were comfortable chairs and personal electronic gear—iPads and other devices to pass the time when the crew members were not on duty. The Ares I module rotated about its axis during the trip to provide a slight g-force so the crew members were not weightless during the voyage.

An airlock at the rear of the crew quarters led to the third section, the cargo hold. On Ares I, it would contain a probe that was to be sent to the surface of Phobos, but on later missions it would carry components for building a manned station on the tiny Martian moon.

The fourth section of the Ares I module consisted of the liquid fuel tanks and rocket engines that would be ignited to propel the vehicle on two occasions. The first would be to launch the Ares I module from its Earth orbit into a trajectory toward Mars. Once inserted into the deep space trajectory, the rocket engines would be shut down and the sail deployed to conserve fuel for the return trip. Prior to entering an orbit around Mars in tandem with Phobos, the sail would be jettisoned.

When the mission tasks had been completed, the vehicle would break out of its orbit and descend toward the surface of Mars, initiating the slingshot maneuver to take advantage of the Martian gravity. The rocket engines would then be fired a second time to break away from Mars and place the Ares I vehicle in its return to Earth trajectory. That burn would continue until the vehicle had been accelerated to more than 36,000 miles per hour—more than double the speed of satellites in Earth orbit—allowing the vehicle to travel the enormous distance home in six months.

Yet, even as Ares I stood nearly ready, Isaiah witnessed the first heavy-lift vehicle arriving with one of the components for a subsequent mission scheduled to follow more than a year later.

Isaiah looked forward to the crew's arrival and vowed all systems on the Ares I module would be in perfect order for the launch scheduled for late February. The Chief Astronaut's deputy arrived a few minutes before the conclusion of Isaiah's duty watch. Isaiah made a few notations in the electronic log and retired to his quarters for a few hours off before he planned to have dinner with Kayla.

Chapter Eleven – Global Technologies

A few minutes before landing, Crawford could see the runway pattern of Hobby Airport in the distance. Located about seven miles from downtown, the airport had opened more than a hundred years before as a private field in a pasture. Currently named for a former Texas Governor, the airport had a storied history, including being known for a brief time as Howard R. Hughes Airport because the famous entrepreneur had been responsible for several major improvements to the airport, including the building of its first tower.

Crawford's flight chirped to a landing, drawing his attention back to his day ahead. He left the plane with a throng of passengers and worked his way to the baggage claim area. A seasoned traveler, Crawford usually traveled with only carry-on luggage, but this time he checked a suitcase with the package inside because he didn't want to be questioned about it by TSA as he boarded the aircraft. Relieved to see the suitcase on the carousel, he grabbed his bag and hurried toward the taxi queue outside.

Hailing the first cab in line, he jumped in. "Global Technologies Towers," he said. Within twenty minutes, the taxi stopped in front of a magnificent building, fifty-seven stories tall and encased in ocean-green glass. A thin, gray obelisk at the very top gave the illusion of pointing to the heavens. Crawford craned his neck to see the top of the spire and then, self-conscious about appearing to be some kind of a rube from the country, lowered his gaze and strode through the building's huge, revolving entry doors. Walking across the floor covered with the finest, grained marble, Crawford stepped into a crowded elevator and felt an extended swoosh as it whisked him to the forty-seventh floor. He showed his I.D. to the guard who checked his validity as a visitor and his appointment time.

The guard nodded to his left. "Room 4719," he said. "You're expected."

Crawford reached the door, knocked and entered after a buzzer signified the lock had been opened. In less than twenty minutes, he reappeared. Before closing the door on the way out, he said, "I'll be back at ten tomorrow morning. Have it ready." Crawford closed the door and took the elevator to the lobby. He left the building, taking a cab to his hotel.

Later that afternoon, Crawford called the Johnson Space Center and asked to be put through to Taylor. When Taylor answered, Crawford explained that he would be in Houston for the following day and that after a business meeting in the morning, he had the afternoon and evening free.

"Would it be possible for me to be scheduled for one of Jaelyn's tours tomorrow? I'd love to see the simulator mockup. My wife's told me so much about it. After the tour, could both of you join me for dinner at the Texan Club?"

Taylor gave Crawford a quick answer. "We'd love to have you join us at the space center and have dinner tomorrow evening. Jaelyn's tour begins at noon. We'd finish in time to beat the afternoon traffic. Do you need a ride to the restaurant?"

"It'd make it a lot simpler if I could tag along with you."

"No problem. We'll see you tomorrow at the center."

Moira Lambert's aide poked his head inside her office. "The communications link you requested has been established. The Chief Astronaut is on the line."

"Is the connection secure?" she asked, reaching for her phone.

"Yes, Ma'am. Patched through Mission Control in Houston and encrypted."

"Thank you. Please close the door behind you," Moira said and then spoke into her phone. "Chief Astronaut Isaiah Wilson?" She detested the delayed echo caused by the satellite link.

"Director Lambert?" came the response.

"Yes. Do you have a few moments?" Moira asked.

"I do, Director Lambert. What can I help you with?"

"To begin with, drop the formalities. I've known you for most of your career, and we've been at several social events together. We are not conversing on open airwaves; this is a private conversation. Titles may be acceptable protocol in public, but today we must communicate person to person, and I am not inclined to hide behind titles. I've always called you Isaiah, and you should call me Moira, or if you're uncomfortable with that, Ms. Lambert. Okay?"

After an extended pause, Isaiah overcame his ingrained military training to address a superior formally and said, "Yes, Ms. Lambert. I'm happy that you call me Isaiah."

"Isaiah, I've been authorized by the FBI to alert you to an issue that could have serious—even disastrous—consequences. The entire subject is classified, and you may not divulge what I'm going to say to anyone—*no one*—is that clear?"

"Very clear, Ms. Lambert."

Satisfied that the Chief Astronaut understood the nature of her communication, Moira explained that the FBI had reason to believe a foreign country was trying, for reasons still unclear, to sabotage the Ares program. It might be Russia, who for some strange reason had been publicly blaming the U.S. for the loss of its probes. Or the Chinese, who might attempt through a cyber attack to gain information on the Higgs-Boson breakthrough in order to weaponize that knowledge. "Or it could simply be terrorism," Moira said. "Whatever the source, I need your help."

"Anything you ask," Isaiah replied.

Moira told him first of all to be alert for any suspicious activity on the station, particularly if related to the Ares program. However, she had a specific request. "I need you to review the personnel files of everyone on duty at the station," she said. "Look for someone who might be receptive to a contact from a hostile interest. A disgruntled employee, or someone passed over for a promotion, or someone politically at odds with the U.S., or even a person who for some reason could be subject to blackmail. A love triangle—anything."

Isaiah thought a long time about Moira's comments. "We have representatives from all six member countries on board. As you know, more than half of those countries are not aligned with the best interests of the U.S."

"I didn't say it would be easy. I said it was imperative that we identify any person who might collaborate with any group having the objective of causing a disaster with the Ares program."

Isaiah told Moira that no one came to mind but promised he would begin the review at once.

"I have fifty-two on board. It'll take a few days to go through all the records. What if I find anything?"

"Call me anytime, day or night. I hope the FBI is wrong, but we cannot take the chance that they are not."

"You have my word, Ms. Lambert. I'll leave no page unread."

"I'm counting on you. Thank you for your service. This conversation is over."

Moira broke the communications link connection and placed the handset of her phone back in its cradle.

Crawford arrived at the Johnson Space Center and greeted Jaelyn and Taylor in the visitor lobby. They whisked him into a waiting shuttle and took him to the simulator laboratory.

"Where are all the others on the tour?" Crawford asked.

"We canceled the normal tour. You're getting the VIP treatment. It's our pleasure," Jaelyn said.

Rather than lead Crawford to the observation room overlooking the Ares I module, the two of them took him instead to a small ante room adjacent to the lab.

"We've got to get you suited up," Jaelyn said. She pointed to a chair and asked Crawford to remove his Stetson and boots. Once done, she handed him booties, latex gloves, and a paper mask. Crawford took a moment and donned the gear.

"All done," he said.

"Not quite," Jaelyn said, handing him a hair net. "It's not as Texas as your Stetson, but it's required in a sterile environment."

Crawford noticed that his two hosts already had donned their own gear in movements made swift by practice. "All this just to go into the lab?" he asked.

"Well, yes," Taylor answered, "but you're going into the command module with us."

That idea pleased Crawford and, unseen behind the mask, he flashed his broad smile.

"Always wanted to be an astronaut," he said.

"Did you ever apply?" Jaelyn asked.

"No. NASA split their britches with me when I was in college at A&M. Never quite got over it. Then of all things, I met and married a woman who ended up in one of the top positions."

"She may get to be administrator before she's done," Jaelyn said. "We all think very highly of your wife."

"What happened between you and NASA, if you don't mind my asking?" Taylor asked.

Crawford chose his words with care. Not many knew the story and he didn't want to cast any aspersions on his wife. "I don't mind. It's been years."

Crawford explained that his dad had approached NASA about providing them a section of land to build a high-gain receiving antenna on his land at the beginning of the U.S. space program. It would be a tracking station for the moonshots. The land was offered at no cost with a ninety-nine year lease. NASA signed a letter of intent, and the word got out, making Crawford's dad a local hero in Amarillo. The townspeople wholeheartedly supported the space program. Every time Crawford's dad went into town to conduct ranch business, people would shake his hand and clap him on the back, congratulating him for his contribution.

"Oh-oh," Taylor said. "NASA backed out, didn't they?"

Crawford hung his head. "Yeah. Something about not being an ideal site. Dad got a terse letter about the withdrawal."

Crawford told of his dad's disappointment and of his difficulty facing his friends in town.

"Dad's health went downhill after that," Crawford said. "Don't know if it was depression or just old age, but he passed away within a year. One of the few pieces of paper I found in his desk when settling his estate was the Letter of Intent from NASA."

"You must have felt terrible," Jaelyn said.

"For a few years I did. NASA was a four-letter word around my house and the townspeople knew better than to bring the subject up with me. But running the ranch kept me busy. And then I met Moira, and, uh . . . well, you know the rest. NASA and I are on good terms, now, thanks to her."

The three entered the lab and approached the Ares I module. Taylor led Crawford up the stairs to the command module entry port. "Jaelyn will go first and sit in my seat on the left side of the second row. You'll go next and sit in the pilot's seat in the front row on the right. I'll sit in front where Andrew will command the module. We don't have any of the systems activated, but you can observe while I point out a few things."

Once all were inside, Taylor closed and locked the hatch, giving Crawford a brief twinge of claustrophobia. Crawford took a few deep, calming breaths and focused his attention on Taylor as he explained the controls and features of the capsule, including the connections for Andrew and the basics of the Higgs-Boson equipment. Crawford experienced a lifetime dream come true. He listened with interest as Taylor described Andrew's role of commander for the flight, including his discussion about the android's connections to the capsule's navigation and control systems and his power supply. When they finished, Crawford crawled out of the capsule and stretched, happy to be able to move about. "One year for your round trip," he said, giving Taylor a hand to help him exit. "How can you stand it?"

Taylor grinned. "We spend most of the time in the crew quarters watching TV while Andy flies the ship."

"Your quarters aren't much larger than the capsule," Crawford said. "I still think you'd all go daffy."

"Two of the three of us at any given time will be sedated. The third person stands watch in case there's a need for us to be awakened. Makes the time go a lot faster."

Their conversation was interrupted by the arrival of Kazuhiro Sora, his attention focused on his ever-present iPad and not noticing them. Startled when the others greeted him, he looked up, then smiled. "Hi! Mr. Rambert," he said.

Crawford, not aware of the running gag, said, "Lambert."

"Sorry."

"No problem," Crawford said. "I'm glad you're here. Do you remember me talking about the trail ride?"

Kazuhiro nodded.

"I'd love to have you join us. Our group starts in Victoria and spends eight days on the road, but, to make it easy on you, you could meet us on the last night before we enter Houston and ride into town with us. All the trail riders meet at the end of their ride in Memorial Park and lots of folks in town dress up in their finest Western gear to celebrate the arrival of the trail riders. That Friday is called 'Go Texan' day. Then on Saturday morning we parade through downtown Houston. Moira will be joining us for the parade. What do you think?"

Kazuhiro fell silent, deep in thought. He hesitated before speaking. "I, uh . . . well, Crawford, I've never been on a horse before."

"Don't worry. I'll bring my gentlest mare, and if for some reason, the two of you don't get along, you can ride in the wagon. But I think you'd enjoy riding a real horse."

Kazuhiro was still reluctant to agree.

Crawford set the hook. "Kaz, I'll even give you a pair of chaps and spurs. Think how you'd look in a complete trail rider's outfit."

Kazuhiro conjured up a mental image of himself riding on a fiery steed, his mount rearing and whinnying in its eagerness to charge forward. He imagined prodding the stallion onward using the spurs that were jangling from his boots jammed into the stirrups. He visualized himself clad in authentic western chaps, a leather vest and gloves. In his fantasy, he wore a bright red kerchief around his neck and clenched a lariat in his teeth, his head topped with his prized Stetson. His long, gray hair flowed from beneath the brim of his hat and swirled in the breeze.

The more he thought about it, the more Kazuhiro warmed to the idea of a trail ride. "You'd teach me how to hold the reins?" he asked.

Crawford reassured Kazuhiro that he would personally get him comfortable with riding by practicing the evening before, just the two of them. "I've worked with a lot of newcomers to horse riding, from my grandchildren to NASA directors. No one's fallen off the horse yet, and I promise you that I won't let you be the first. But in the end, it'll be your choice—the horse or the wagon."

Kazuhiro broke out in a huge smile and laughed. "Okay, count me in," he said, "but during the ride, you have to call me by a western nickname instead of Kaz."

"Got anything in mind?"

"Rawhide."

Now it was Crawford's turn to laugh. "After your first day in the saddle, that name might be a whole lot more appropriate than you think, but 'Rawhide' it is, pardner."

That evening, Taylor drove Jaelyn and Crawford to the Texan Club on the shore of Galveston Bay at Kemah, a short distance from the space center. They had invited Kazuhiro Sora to join them, but he begged off, saying he had an evening's work planned. Looking forward to one of the best seafood dinners in Houston, the three hurried to the club entrance, their shoes clunking on the rough-hewn boardwalk. When they entered the club's lobby, the receptionist gave them menus and escorted them to their table.

"Oops," Crawford said, still wearing his sun glasses in the darkened interior. "I left my regular glasses in your car."

Taylor offered to retrieve them, but Crawford waved him off. "I'll get them. Lend me your keys, and you two go ahead and order drinks while I'm gone—I'll take a vodka tonic."

Taylor tossed his set of keys to Crawford, and he caught them in midair with a jangle. "Back in a minute," Crawford said before disappearing outside. Once he reached the car, Crawford opened the back door on the side away from the restaurant. He grabbed the case containing his glasses from its position on the rear seat, but with his other hand he withdrew the twenty-seven pin connector he had picked up that morning. With a swift motion, Crawford removed the original connector from Taylor's key chain and replaced it with the one from his own pocket. After a brief exam to satisfy himself that the two connectors looked identical, he stuffed Taylor's connector into his pocket and returned to the restaurant.

Inside the crowded dining area, he spotted Taylor and Jaelyn at a table and rejoined them, returning the key chain to Taylor. "Thanks," Crawford said. He lifted his glass in a toast to the others. "Cheers."

★ ★ ★

The next morning, Moira Lambert answered the buzz from her intercom.

"The Chief Astronaut is on the line," her aide said.

"Secure?"

"Yes."

Moira picked up the handset and answered, "Moira Lambert."

"Chief Astronaut Isaiah Wilson, here, Ms. Lambert."

"Go ahead."

"I've completed my review and need to give you some information."

"Thank you for your promptness. What have you learned?"

"Nothing certain, but I'll let you decide whether it's critical," Isaiah said. "I identified two Russians who might be a possibility, but we've known about them for a long time, and they have been closely monitored. If they were to do anything out of line, we'd know about it. We'll continue to keep them under tight scrutiny."

Moira frowned, worried that Isaiah had turned up no real leads. "Anything else?" she asked.

"Well, there is one thing, but I don't want to get anyone into trouble without any evidence of wrongdoing."

"Isaiah, tell me. You must have confidence that I will do the right thing."

The line remained silent for a time. Then Isaiah began talking again. He told Moira about an astronaut at the station who had been in line for the first Ares mission but who had been passed over. "For a slight disability," Isaiah said. "He injured his left hand playing college football and lost some dexterity in his index and middle fingers. Nothing significant, but enough to let him be edged out by Pilot Brady Owen for the first mission. Worse, he got relegated to backup status. He might fly only if someone were to have to drop out."

"What's he like?"

"One of my best people. I've never heard a word of resentment, and he performs every task I've given him in an excellent manner. He is a key person on the team checking out the Ares module."

"Do you trust him?"

"Explicitly. But you said you wanted the names of anyone who might have a motive. Being denied a flight on the Phobos mission is a major disappointment for someone who worked their whole life to qualify. I'm telling you this because he could have a motive and he does have access—not because I suspect him."

"Thank you, Isaiah," Moira said. "Would you give me his name?"

"Edward Matthew."

Moira scribbled the name on her notepad and ended the call, expressing her gratitude for the information and then adding, "Please do nothing obvious, but keep your eyes open for his activities. Call me immediately if you notice anything out of the ordinary."

"I will."

Chapter Twelve – Diplomacy

Unannounced and without bothering to knock, NASA Administrator Robert Durand with Jerome Mosby in tow, charged into Moira's office. Shocked, she rose to greet them, but Durand cut her short.

"Get your coat. My car will be waiting for us out front. We've been asked to meet with the Secretary of State."

Moira donned her coat and asked, "What about?"

"I'll brief you on the way over. The other two senior directors are out of town. We're trying to connect them by video conference."

Moira didn't care for the smirk on Jerome Mosby's face. *He knows something*, she thought.

Durand's limo awaited them at the curb, and the uniformed driver held the doors as the three entered and sat behind the partition. Durand took a seat by himself facing forward. Moira and Jerome sat across from him. "State Department," Durand said to his driver who began working through D.C. traffic on snowy streets to reach the Harry S Truman building. Whisking through security, the three took an elevator to a conference room adjacent to the secretary's office and were removing their coats when Secretary of State Cal Maxon entered and greeted them all.

They exchanged pleasantries while an aide finished setting up the video conference feed and checked the volume levels. "Everything's ready," he said and left, closing the door behind him. The pleasantries ceased.

"I won't waste your time," Maxon said. "The Russian prime minister is meeting with the president next week, and as if things weren't bad enough, the prime minister is pissed that—according to him—we've destroyed Russia's *Fobos* probes using electronic warfare. He is demanding we make a public admission of our accountability for those actions and pay the Russians restitution for the lost probes."

Moira's expression did not reflect the shock she experienced from hearing the secretary's statement. Nor did the others. Moira expected that the revelation came as no surprise to the administrator, but she couldn't tell if Jerome had already known or whether he was masking his surprise, too.

But the secretary continued. "We've learned through back channels that unless we do as the Russians request, they plan to retaliate by disrupting our Ares program in some manner."

He paused, letting that soak in. A frown crossed his face, and he leaned toward Administrator Durand. "I have to brief the president tomorrow morning on our position on this issue so he can prepare for his meeting with the prime minister. I don't have the goddamned time to be pleasant. What the hell is going on at NASA? And I don't want any bullshit."

Robert Durand remained calm, but spoke in clipped tones. He reminded the secretary that Russia had lost a total of four probes en route to Phobos. In the eighties, they lost contact with the first two as they approached an orbit with Phobos in tandem with each other. Durand said that conspiracy theorists, after reviewing a partial video sent back by the second probe before contact was lost, concluded the video showed unnatural formations on the satellite's surface and a strange shadow that could only be explained as a UFO. The third probe was lost years later shortly after leaving Earth orbit. The only success had been the fourth probe ten years ago, but the results of that probe still remained cloaked in secrecy.

"But as you no doubt remember, Russia lost touch with its fifth probe a few months ago," Durand said. "We believe Russia is taking a hard line against the U.S. to cover up their humiliation for these unexplained losses."

The secretary sat back in his chair and folded his hands in front of his chest while he contemplated the answer. "That won't cut it," he said, shaking his head. "There's more." Maxon explained that Russia believes NASA learned from its unmanned Martian landers—Rover, Odyssey, and others—that Phobos and even Deimos are artificial satellites put in orbit by extraterrestrials, confirming the theories suggested by Carl Sagan and even an American astronaut. The Russians are certain that NASA is withholding the knowledge from the general public and worse, maintain that the U.S. has intentionally destroyed the Russian probes to keep Russia from exposing the deception.

"So, the question on the table is: do we know whether Phobos is artificial or not?" the secretary asked.

"We don't," the NASA Administrator answered, "but—"

"Don't waffle," the secretary interrupted.

"—one of the objectives of the Ares program is to determine the answer to that very question. The Higgs-Boson equipment will analyze the unusual formations to determine whether they are natural or not, and we are sending a probe to the surface of the satellite to confirm that it is a captured asteroid—and nothing more."

The answer did not placate the secretary. "Gentlemen," he said, and nodding to Moira, "and lady. I have only a few minutes left with you this morning. I need to know what the hell the president should say to the prime minister next week."

An awkward silence followed his question. Moira cleared her throat and stepped in. "The president should tell him the truth," she said.

Maxon turned his head and stared at her. "And that is—?" he asked.

May as well go all in, Moira thought and answered without hesitation. "The U.S. had no role in the destruction of the Russian probes. We will not offer restitution nor will we discontinue the Ares program."

"What if you delayed the program a few months to let this issue settle down?"

Moira shook her head. "Our launch window is dictated by the relative position of Mars to Earth. It won't be as close again until more than a year later. Remember, we're sending the first two crew members to the International Space Station in three weeks followed by the other two members a week later. Launch of the Ares I module is scheduled for March 15."

"The Ides of March? Aren't you concerned about that timing? Launching a mission to Phobos—named for fear—that orbits Mars—the Roman god of war—on a date Caesar was assassinated?"

"No. Science governs our timing—not superstition or mythology."

The secretary shifted his focus. "What about the question of whether or not Phobos is artificial?"

"We have no knowledge that it is. Although rumors about it being artificial have grown into an urban legend, we believe that possibility would be unlikely. Our Ares program is one of scientific exploration, however, to determine answers to that—and other—questions."

"What if you found—unlikely as it might be—that Phobos *is* artificial?"

Jerome Mosby enjoyed watching the trap spring on Moira, knowing she was not in a position to decide the course of action were that to be the case. The NASA Administrator assumed control. "NASA works for the White House," he said. "If we were to gain that knowledge, I would make a direct report to the president and not divulge it to anyone else. What to do in that instance is the sole responsibility of the president."

Durand's answer seemed to satisfy Maxon. The secretary's mood lightened as he contemplated Durand's response. "Well, if you're right, we're not going to have anything to worry about. If you're wrong, well . . . the issue becomes bigger than all of us." Maxon checked his watch. "Oh-oh, I'm late. Thanks for meeting with me. I'll let you know if I need anything more."

In the limo on the way back, Robert Durand, who was a leader not known for passing out compliments, said, "Good job in there, Moira."

"Thanks," she said. She enjoyed watching the feigned expression of inattention on Jerome Mosby's face. *Had the administrator held back his answer to Maxon on purpose to see how the rest of us might handle the question? Durand's recommendation about his replacement would carry a lot of weight,* she thought. Moira touched the red sapphire stone in the pin she wore on her jacket and smiled.

Ashlyn and Jaelyn were both home in their apartment at the same time, a rarity. Each had different plans for the evening, but they were enjoying the morning with each other catching up on household chores and jabbering back and forth. The twins got along exceptionally well, and each had no better friend than the other.

Ashlyn busied herself in their small office, sorting through the stack of bills and other papers on a cluttered desk. The hum of the vacuum in the hall stopped, and Jaelyn stepped into the office.

"We need to talk," Jaelyn said.

Ashlyn turned and gave her twin her undivided attention. "What about?"

Jaelyn plopped down in an overstuffed chair and exhaled. "I'm not sure how to start."

"Something's bothering you. We've always been able to confide in each other. What is it?"

Jaelyn got up and took a step to leave. Changing her mind, she sat back down on the chair's armrest.

"This is different," she said. "It's about the mission."

Ashlyn felt a bit of relief about the topic. "No need to worry about the mission. We both know what the risks are. We've accepted them."

"I wish it were only about that."

"For God's sake, Jaelyn. Stop leading me on. Out with it."

It took a moment for Jaelyn to begin speaking, but once she began, the words flowed quickly. "Ever since that day in the lab—you know, the day . . . uh, the day when you experienced my own innermost desires about Taylor. I've thought about you and him spending more than a year together in, uh . . . very close quarters."

Ashlyn walked across the room and put her arm around her sister's shoulder. "You have nothing to worry about. I am in no way attracted to Taylor, close quarters or not. Do you really think anything X-rated is going to happen with a third person—plus a robot—looking on? Not to mention all the prying ears back at Mission Control?"

"I'm not worried about you. I'm worried about Taylor. What if he sees you as a surrogate for me, your twin? What if he comes on to you?"

Ashlyn laughed. "Jaelyn, I'm your older sister—by seven minutes—believe me, I can handle Taylor. And besides, with the Higgs-Boson equipment on board, you'll always know in your own mind what's going on. Stop worrying. It isn't going to happen."

Jaelyn hugged her twin. Neither spoke for a moment. Then Ashlyn broke the mood. "I've never been called a surrogate before. That's a new one."

Once back at the executive suite at the NASA headquarters, the administrator disappeared into his office, but Jerome Mosby lagged behind, waiting to have a few words with Moira. While she removed her coat and turned on her computer, Mosby stood, leaning against the door jamb.

"So now you're advising presidents?" he said.

"No one spoke up," Moira said. "You had your chance."

Mosby took a few steps toward Moira and lowered his voice. "The questions the secretary was asking were related to my operations, not yours. You need to stick to your own territory."

Moira brushed by Mosby and slammed her office door. She turned and faced him head on. "You're the one who needs to stick to your own territory. I told you before, and I'll repeat it now. Keep your nose out of my business."

Mosby didn't back down. "I'm not the only one with a nose in your business. I understand the FBI is breathing down your neck. And then there's the issue with your husband."

Moira should have known the FBI's presence would not have remained confidential, but she got caught off guard by the comment about Crawford. "What do you mean by that inane comment?"

Mosby pressed on, certain he had gained the upper hand. "The last time I looked at the organization chart, I couldn't find his name listed as a NASA employee. Yet he keeps showing up in the most privileged situations. Let's see, there was his presence in your leadership session, and later, a private dinner with Kazuhiro Sora. I heard he had a personal tour inside the Ares I module, including an overview about how all the equipment functioned. A dinner with an astronaut and our two twins—need I go on?"

Moira fumed. Several of the examples were new to her. *I warned Crawford to be careful about perceptions*, she thought. "He's my husband, for Christ's sake. He's done nothing wrong. And if there were anything at all to support your allegations, I'd know it first and be on top of it."

"I'm sure you would, Ms. Lambert," Mosby said. "But just to let you know, there are others who have noticed."

That did it. Moira opened her door and escorted Mosby out, grabbing his elbow and giving him an assist. *Know-it-all bastard,* she seethed. But Mosby's comments were worrisome and had gotten under her skin.

Chapter Thirteen – Rawhide

On the frigid last day of February, Kazuhiro Sora picked his way through rush hour traffic to Sugarland, a town on the western outskirts of Houston named for the old Imperial Sugar factory. Before long, he came upon the gate leading into an open field that Crawford had described. A banner above the gate proclaimed the occupants to be "Victoria Trail Riders."

Once inside, Kazuhiro felt he had traveled in time to a long forgotten era. A temporary corral held dozens of horses, the foggy vapors from their nostrils visible as they snorted and whinnied. Scattered throughout the field were wagons and buckboards silhouetted against the flickering lights from a dozen smoky campfires. People in authentic western gear—adults and children—were gathered around a central barbeque smoker that appeared to be about the size of a small locomotive.

Everyone had a plate in hand and a cup of their favorite beverage, from soft drinks for the kids to beer and wine for the adults. The kids were chasing each other and shouting, playing a game of tag while the cooks prepared the food.

The aroma of mesquite-smoked brisket, ribs, and chicken wafted through the encampment, teasing Kazuhiro's hunger pangs. He parked his car near the gate and sauntered through the field, eager to show off his boots and hat, but chilled by the damp, evening air. Trying to spot Crawford, he had to ward off constant interruptions by strangers welcoming him and offering him a plate and eating utensils. Over the commotion, he heard a shout and saw a man at the center of the crowd at the barbecue pit wave to him. "Hey, Rawhide! Over here," the man shouted. Kazuhiro recognized Crawford's voice.

Happy to see a familiar face, Kazuhiro waved back and took large, but awkward, strides toward his friend. After twisting his ankle when he stepped into a hoof print, he hid a grimace from the pain and reached Crawford who clapped him on the back and welcomed him to the trail ride.

"Come on, let's get the rest of your gear, and we can practice some riding before it gets dark," Crawford said, handing Kazuhiro a mug filled with beer. Crawford rummaged around in his wagon and withdrew several articles of western clothing—leather chaps, a vest, and a set of spurs.

"Try these," Crawford said, motioning for Kazuhiro to sit on an upturned stump while strapping on the spurs. Once finished—but only after needing some assistance—Kazuhiro stood and took a few steps, enjoying the jangle that accompanied each stride. He cinched the belt of the chaps around his waist, and after fumbling a time with the leg straps, managed to get them on. He fastened the vest but left the bottom two snaps open for comfort. Kazuhiro looked for a mirror to check his image, but before he could find one, Crawford led him to a horse tethered to the rear of the wagon. Crawford patted the horse's nose and handed her a sugar cube. The horse swallowed the cube and nuzzled Crawford's vest pocket, looking for more.

"Name's Sophie," Crawford said. He handed Kazuhiro a sugar cube. "You try giving her one."

Kazuhiro took a tentative step toward Sophie, holding the cube in the outstretched palm of his hand. Sophie nibbled the cube, and Kazuhiro withdrew his hand, a bit unnerved by the feel of the horse's velveteen lips on his palm and the sight of Sophie's long teeth. Sophie nuzzled Kazuhiro's chest, too, nearly knocking him off balance.

Crawford, laughed. "You did great. No need to worry, she's my gentlest mare."

Crawford loosened the reins from the wagon and handed the ends to Kazuhiro. "I'll give you a leg up," he said, and clasped his hands together by interlocking his fingers and rested them on his knee. "Reins in your left hand. Both hands on the saddle horn. Left foot in my hands and when you're ready, step up and I'll give you a boost."

The first time it didn't work right, and Kazuhiro slid off of Sophie's back, hanging onto the saddle in a desperate effort to avoid stumbling to the ground.

"Sorry," he said.

"Don't worry, Rawhide. It happens to the best. Let's try again."

This time Kazuhiro made it and lurched into the saddle, his body askew. Crawford guided his left leg into the stirrup. "Just the toes," he said. He then steadied Kazuhiro while he swung his right leg forward, trying to locate the stirrup. After a couple of attempts, he succeeded.

"Feel secure?" Crawford asked.

Kazuhiro nodded, hiding his apprehension.

"Hand me the reins," Crawford said. "You hang on to the saddle horn, and we'll walk around a bit."

Crawford eased the reins over Sophie's head and led the mare in a gentle walk. He saw Kazuhiro hunched over, squeezing the saddle horn with white knuckles and pressing his knees into the mare's sides with a grimace frozen on his face.

"Relax. I'm not going to let you fall off," Crawford said. "You'll get used to it in a minute."

Crawford walked Sophie a few yards and turned back toward the wagon. With each step, Kazuhiro loosened his grasp on the saddle horn, and his grimace began to fade. Reaching the wagon again, Crawford stopped and handed Kazuhiro the reins. He showed him how to turn the horse in either direction and how to rein her to a stop. Crawford walked Sophie again, leading her by the bridle, keeping a close eye on his student. "Looking good,

Rawhide!" he said. "A few more times up and back, and you'll be ready to try it on your own."

Kazuhiro's mouth became dry. This experience was not at all the dashing adventure he had envisioned. He felt it was more a question of survival.

Crawford stopped and handed Kazuhiro the reins again. "I'll walk beside you to give you any help if you need it, but I think you'll do fine."

Kazuhiro and Sophie stood, not moving, frozen like a statue. After a moment, Crawford told Kazuhiro to move his left hand forward with the reins to encourage Sophie to move. "Click your tongue," he said. "But don't you dare use your spurs—they're just decorations for now."

Kazuhiro clicked his tongue, and Sophie began walking forward, jouncing him in the saddle, each jolt shifting his body toward the side. "Whoa," Crawford said, stopping Sophie. "Get centered in the saddle and try again."

Kazuhiro tried it again but had the same result. Once more, Crawford stopped the horse. "You know those particles you accelerate in your collider?" Crawford asked.

Kazuhiro nodded.

"Well, I don't know near as much about them as you do, but I know horses, and there are some similarities."

"What do you mean?"

"Simple. To accelerate your particles, you have to move them with alternating magnets, don't you?"

"Yes, synchronized."

"That's right. Your collider wouldn't work if the magnets weren't in sync with the particles, would it?"

"No."

"Well, neither does horse riding. You have to be in sync with the motions of the horse. You can't fight them. When you fight a horse's stride, you bounce."

Kazuhiro thought about it, never dreaming there would be a parallel between particle colliders and horse riding. But the analogy made some sense. "What do I need to do?" he asked.

"Loosen up. You're so tense, you're out of sync. Enjoy it instead. Now, let's try again."

This time, after a few steps, Kazuhiro eased into the saddle, in sync with Sophie's gate. A feeling came over him like he had shifted into second gear and he and Sophie were one.

"You've got it, Rawhide," Crawford said. "Now, I'll stay here, and you walk her to the fence and come back."

Crawford watched with the apprehension of a dad letting his son ride a bicycle for the first time. But Kazuhiro did well, even turning the horse around with ease. On the way back, Crawford watched him sitting erect in the saddle with a huge grin on his face. He reined Sophie in and dismounted without assistance, pleasing Crawford. "Way to go, Rawhide. You've earned your spurs. In the parade tomorrow, Sophie will be well behaved, and you'll ride next to me. It'll be easier than what you've done tonight," Crawford said. "Now let's go get some brisket, chili, and another beer. We can talk more around the fire. I want to hear all the latest about your project."

An hour before dawn the next morning, while the trail riders were wolfing down a breakfast of bacon, sausage, and flapjacks, a half a continent away at the Kennedy Space Center the mammoth doors of the Vehicle Assembly Building opened, gliding silently along steel rails.

Inside, bathed in floodlights, stood the assembled Eagle 2M two-stage vehicle that would lift Pilot Brady Owen and Mission Specialist Ashlyn Johnson to the International Space Station. The

Eagle capsule would return to Earth, flown by Edward Matthew and another astronaut, so that the capsule could be mated with the first stage that had been recovered from a previous flight and refurbished for reuse. Andrew would pilot the second launch of the Eagle 2M craft to take him and Mission Specialist Taylor Carson to the station. Inside Mission Control in Houston, all four watched the proceedings on a live video feed.

At nearly the height of a thirty-story building and weighing four million pounds, the Eagle 2M craft, atop an enormous platform on a crawler, began its ten-hour trek along the crawler path to Launch Complex 39B. Once used for shuttle launches, the complex had been modified by Apogee Systems, Inc. for use in Eagle launches.

The sight of the rocket, appearing in the morning darkness like a white candlestick cradled in a holder, brought chills to the observing crew members.

"In ten days, we'll be aboard," Ashlyn said to Brady. "Years of preparation—successes and disappointments—and now it's becoming a reality."

"You think this feeling is powerful. Just wait until we get to the station and board the Ares ship," Brady said. "We're the first humans going to another planet."

Andrew jumped in. "Humans? What about me?"

Ashlyn giggled.

"Quiet, Andrew," Taylor said. "Just a figure of speech. Besides, I thought you wanted to be treated as a human anyway. Take it as a compliment."

"Since you brought the subject up, are you going to invite me to your party next Friday, the night before your pre-launch curfew begins?"

"No, Andrew. We've been over and over that before. NASA would fire us all if we took you to some bar and got you banged up. The rest of us all have backups, but you're one of a kind—you're irreplaceable."

"It's no fun being irreplaceable."

Kazuhiro Sora finished his second helping of flapjacks, looking forward to the trail ride into Houston. Crawford gathered the plates and utensils and washed them in a pan full of water. He squinted toward the eastern horizon, looking for the first rays of sunrise.

"You ready, Rawhide?"

Kazuhiro nodded.

In an eerie parallel to Eagle 2M's journey to the launch pad, the trail ride would take about ten hours to reach its destination. Rather than being bathed in spotlights, the riders would be escorted by highway patrol cars, flashing red and blue lights ablaze. All the trail riders would converge on Houston's Memorial Park, coming from all directions, following routes like spokes on a wagon wheel. Crowds, dressed in western gear, were already beginning to line the roadways to cheer the riders on.

One of Crawford's ranch hands brought two horses from the corral and began hitching the team to the wagon. Another hand brought Sophie and a beautiful stallion for Crawford. The hand saddled Sophie for Kazuhiro, but Crawford saddled his own.

"In our group, I'll lead and you ride next to me on Sophie. She'll know what to do, since she's done this every year for ten years. One of my hands will follow us in my wagon and the other will drive my cart in case we need it. Got it?"

Again Kazuhiro nodded, this time some anxiety building within himself.

The notes of a bugle broke the pre-dawn silence, a signal for the riders to mount up. Whoops and cheers arose from the riders as they mounted their horses to begin the final segment of the ride.

"Here you go," Crawford said, giving Kazuhiro a leg up, then mounting his own horse. Crawford unfurled an American flag and inserted the staff into a holder on his left stirrup. Kazuhiro grabbed his Stetson and swung it in a circle above his head. Beside himself with excitement and anticipation, he let out a yell that surprised even Crawford.

The bugle sounded the cavalry notes of "charge," and with a bustle of activity, the riders began moving.

"Let's go, Rawhide!" Crawford said. "You'll have no more memorable day in your life than this!"

Isaiah Wilson stood in the air lock by the open hatch for the Ares I module, nodding his head to three assembly technicians as they exited the capsule. He then entered and met astronaut Edward Matthew inside the crew quarters, who held a sheaf of documents in his hands.

"Final integrity inspections complete," Eddie said, handing Isaiah the papers. "Here are the certifications."

Isaiah took the documents and reviewed them, page by page. He stared at Eddie, searching for any sign of nervousness or hesitation. "No issues?" he asked.

"None. This bird's ready to fly. I wish I were going."

"Walk me through. I'll sign off on each system as you review it for me."

The two men went through the module from front to back, double checking the craft's integrity. For each critical point in the system, Eddie gave an overview of the checks that he and the assembly technicians had performed. After questioning the astronaut about each system and once satisfied by his answers, Isaiah signed the certification paper for that system. The process took several hours, but when finished, Isaiah knew for certain the vehicle was ready for flight.

The two men exited the module and used the complex locking mechanism to close the hatch. Once outside, Isaiah placed his seal on the door, assuring the module would remain sterile until the crew members were allowed to enter later that week.

Isaiah and Eddie worked their way through the corridors and portals of the station, Isaiah heading for the bridge and Eddie to the station's crew quarters. Before they parted, Isaiah hesitated a moment. "You're taking the Eagle 2M capsule back to the surface next week after the first of the crew members arrive. If the pilot for some reason were to have to cancel, would you be ready and most important, willing, to take over for them?" Isaiah again watched Ed's expression and body language for any clue suggesting a reluctance to answer.

"I wouldn't wish anything bad to happen to anyone, but if it did, I'd jump at the chance."

"No reservations about the ship?"

"None. Would I have signed the papers if I had any?"

Isaiah put his hand on the astronaut's shoulder. "And I'd go with you if I could."

He turned to leave. The astronaut spoke to him. "And I'd ride with you, too. Maybe someday we'll both get the chance."

Isaiah walked away, satisfied that his trust in Eddie had been validated.

The trail riders passed through the entry gate and proceeded onto the highway, traffic blocked in either direction by state troopers who stood beside their patrol cars, waving at the participants. When Crawford passed the troopers, they snapped to attention and saluted the flag he carried. Once all the riders were on the shoulder of the highway and headed towards town, the troopers got in their cars, one taking the lead and the other bringing up the rear, lights on both cars flashing. Even Houston commuters, driving to work in the morning rush, gave the riders enthusiastic waves, appreciating the Texas heritage on display.

Kazuhiro Sora enjoyed hearing the clop-clop-clop of the metal horseshoes on the pavement and the metallic rumble of the steel rims on the wagon wheels. People in passing cars often shouted encouragement. "Sometimes they'll honk. That's why I want you riding next to me on the outside, away from the cars. You and Sophie will both be more comfortable in that case."

The miles went on and on. The procession, aided by the troopers, passed through traffic light controlled intersections, and navigated through cavernous overpasses and over railroad crossings. After a few hours, Kazuhiro's excitement waned. His back ached. Worse, he felt the beginnings of chafing burns on his inner thighs, calves, and buttocks—anywhere his body touched the saddle. He squirmed and shifted his weight, trying to find a position that would relieve the burning.

By noon the riders had reached the halfway point and stopped in a parking lot, roped off for them, for a quick lunch and bathroom break. Crawford helped Kazuhiro dismount and watched him gingerly walk toward the chuck wagon for a sandwich, rubbing his behind. Crawford caught up with him in line. "How are you doing, Rawhide?" he asked.

"I'm getting pretty sore."

Crawford chuckled. "Now you know where the term, 'rawhide,' comes from, don't you?"

Kazuhiro nodded.

"Tell you what, my friend. We'll save your butt for the parade tomorrow when Moira joins us. Why don't you ride in the wagon the rest of the way today?"

Kazuhiro thought a moment. "You won't be disappointed in me?"

"Of course not. You've done much better than I expected, and I don't want you to miss out on all the hoopla tomorrow."

"Thank God."

Chapter Fourteen – Party

Late that Friday afternoon, eleven trail rides consisting of more than 500 riders and untold numbers of livestock converged upon Memorial Park, wending their way through streets lined with onlookers and navigating through a gauntlet of television reporters. City officials glad-handed the dismounting riders and competed for air time to promote their own agendas. Soon, the cool, evening air was laden with layers of blue smoke emanating from barbecue pits and campfires.

Kazuhiro Sora remained seated on the wagon, too stiff and sore to lend a hand with tethering the horses. Crawford climbed aboard and sat next to him. "The parade starts at eleven tomorrow morning. I'll be riding with Moira, but the golf cart is ready for you—the cushions are pretty soft."

"Thanks, Crawford. If you don't mind, I'm going to pass on dinner and the partying tonight."

"I understand, Rawhide. There's a bedroll for you in the wagon. I, uh . . . well I hope the trail ride didn't interfere with your priorities next week—the launch to the space station and all."

"I wouldn't have missed it. The chance of a lifetime. I can't wait for the parade tomorrow. As for the mission, my duties are done until the Ares I crew leaves the station for Phobos. Up to then, I'm just an observer."

"So this H-B experiment you're working on, it's all ready?"

"Yes."

"How do you monitor the progress?"

"I'll be at the Johnson Space Center with Jaelyn performing experiments. I'll be watching a live video feed from the capsule, but Jaelyn won't be able to see it. She'll be connected to the capsule only by mental telepathy from her sister."

A beer cart, pulled by a pony, passed the wagon. Crawford flagged them down for a beer.

"Want one?" he asked Kazuhiro.

"Yeah, maybe it'll dull some of my aches."

Crawford signaled for two and grabbed the frosty mugs overflowing with foam. Giving one to his friend, he clinked the mugs and offered a toast. "Here's to a successful mission." Both men took a few swigs. Crawford wiped the foam from his moustache. "Will the public be able to view your video feed?"

"Oh, no. It's encrypted. The science is proprietary, and there are too many of our enemies who would love to weaponize our knowledge. We can't risk the technology falling into the wrong hands."

Crawford finished his beer. "Another?" he asked.

Kazuhiro shook his head. "I'm calling it a night."

Across town, another party had begun. Pilot Brady Owen and mission specialists Taylor Carson and the twins, Jaelyn and Ashlyn Johnson, were at a table at a sports bar. Their curfew began the next day so it would be the last night they could party before the mission. Several rounds of empty glasses were spread about the table in front of them and peanut hulls from a half-empty bucket littered the floor. The four of them were kidding back and forth, not mentioning anything about the forthcoming mission for the sake of confidentiality. Jaelyn sat close to Taylor, pressing her leg against his, apprehensive about his forthcoming departure. Brady and Ashlyn had no such qualms and both had already had enough to drink that they felt no pain.

Taylor squeezed Jaelyn's knee and excused himself to leave for the restroom. "Back soon," he said.

He had been gone a minute or two when the door to the bar opened and Jaelyn, who sat facing the door said, "Uh-oh! Look who just came in."

The others turned to see the reason for her exclamation and caught sight of Andrew entering the room. He wore a jacket and had a cap pulled down over his head to be easily mistaken in the dim interior for human. The android spotted them and hurried to join them at their table. "Hi, guys," he said, as if nothing were out of the ordinary about his presence.

"Hey, Andrew," Brady said. "You need a girl." Brady looked toward the bar and saw a pretty woman seated by herself. "Go invite her to our table," he said, jabbing an elbow in Ashlyn's side and giving her a sly wink.

Andrew didn't hesitate. He stepped to the bar and sat next to the woman, engaging her in conversation.

When Taylor returned to the table, he saw the others watching something going on at the bar. Taylor nearly fell over when he saw the object of their attention. "Jesus," he said, "How did he get here?"

Taylor rushed to the bar to pull Andrew aside, but he didn't make it in time. A man returned to the empty stool on the opposite side of the woman and saw his date talking with a stranger. "Leave her alone," he yelled.

Andrew blinked, not understanding why the man would be so rude. The man bristled up and approached Andrew. "Get your ass out of here," he said.

Andrew tried to be polite. "But she and I were talking."

Taylor started to jump between them, but the man swung his fist at Andrew's jaw, connecting with a clanking sound of flesh and bone against metal. The man grabbed his wrist and screamed in pain. Taylor grabbed Andrew's elbow, pulling him away from the fight and stepping between him and the stranger.

"It's okay," Taylor said to the man. "He's drunk. He didn't mean anything. I'll take him home."

The man glared at Taylor, still grimacing in pain. "What the hell did I hit?"

"He's wearing a neck brace under his collar. Sorry."

The stranger backed off and returned to his seat. Taylor escorted Andrew toward the door, passing the others at the table. "I'll deal with all of you later. The success of our whole mission rides on a billion dollar piece of technology that you let get into a bar fight. Damn it, what were you thinking?"

Jaelyn rushed to Taylor's side and the three of them left, with Taylor still wondering how Andrew had awakened from hibernation. He planned to run a complete diagnostic program on the android once they got him back to the center.

That evening, Moira joined the trail riders encamped at the park. Having flown in from D.C. and dressed in business attire, she looked a bit out of place compared to the rest of the riders, most of whom had been on the road for more than a week. But they all knew her from her numerous trail rides with them and overlooked her appearance. In no time, Moira took a seat on a hay bale with Crawford. Kazuhiro stood next to them, all three enjoying the barbecue, beer, and the fellowship of the riders.

A few minutes after darkness settled, Moira clapped her hands to gain the attention of the entire group. Glancing her watch, she stood by the campfire and spoke. "Watch the western sky. In a few minutes, the International Space Station will appear above the horizon, and tonight it will fly directly overhead. Next week, the first team of our astronauts will be launched from the Cape to dock with the station, followed by the second team a few days later. Two weeks from tonight Ares I will begin its journey to Phobos."

All eyes turned toward the western sky, and at the precise moment predicted, a brilliant star—shining brighter than even

Venus—appeared and arced overhead. The riders were awed by the sight and were unprepared for the ethereal connections to the phenomena they experienced—the Old West of Texas to the gleaming space station; humans on Earth to those in orbit aboard the station; and trail riders enjoying a friendship with a NASA leader in great part responsible for the daring mission to come.

Moira raised her glass and proposed a toast. "To the men and women aboard the station and to those soon to be joining them, we pray for their safety and wish them Godspeed."

Cheers of "Here! Here!" and "Amen!" came from the riders, capped off by a few enthusiastic whoops of "Yee Haws" rising into the night sky.

When the excitement had died down, Crawford turned to Kazuhiro and said, "Well, Rawhide. Last night you bunked in the wagon, but Moira will join me there tonight. So, you're going to get the authentic experience of the old cowboys on the prairie by sleeping in a bedroll next to the campfire. Think you can handle that, fella?"

Kazuhiro nodded, happy to be able to curl up anywhere and rest his sore butt.

Taylor asked Andrew to sit on the table outside his storage compartment. The two had not spoken a word on the trip back to the simulator lab. "Take your shirt off, Andy. I'm going to run a diagnostic program on you and be certain nothing's wrong."

Andrew remained silent while Taylor inserted the twenty-seven pin connector into the port where a human's belly button would be located. Taylor initiated the data download, not bothering to shut Andrew off. "You may feel a few twinges, but we need to talk. I have two questions for you."

Andrew knew he was in trouble. "What are they?"

"Okay, pal. How did you start yourself up and get to the bar?"

Andrew explained the self-starting, electronic shunt he had designed and installed without anyone knowing. "Then I took a cab," he said. "I used the cash from the coffee kitty for the fare."

Taylor hesitated, troubled by Andrew's actions and yet at the same time amazed by his ingenuity. He didn't want to reprimand his friend. It would do no good to damage the bond between them.

Andrew asked, "What is your second question?"

Taylor explained that everyone connected to the mission must have complete trust in the others. "We're all striving for the success of the mission together," he said. "We have to count on every member of the team to do their job to the very best of their abilities."

Andrew began to hang his head. "I know," he said.

"Then how could you risk the entire mission by pulling such a stupid trick?"

Taylor's question cut deep. Andrew took some time before he answered.

"Because I wanted to experience what it was like to be human."

The answer stunned Taylor. Neither said anything until a small beep indicated the diagnostic data had finished being downloaded. Taylor inserted the portable drive into his computer to view the results.

"It'll be fine," Andrew said. "Like always before."

The computer monitor displayed schematics of Andrew's circuitry, and Taylor tabbed through the pages, one by one. All showed green until a page showed up with a section of the circuitry colored yellow.

"You've got a suspicious area here," Taylor said, pointing to the screen.

Andrew stared at it. "That's where I inserted the shunt," he said. "Everything else is fine."

Taylor told Andy that the shunt would have to be removed before the flight to the station. Andrew agreed to have it done. "Are we okay?" he asked Taylor.

Taylor smiled and told Andy they were. "You're not the first astronaut who has done something stupid, myself included, and you probably won't be the last. You see, we're all human. And you truly learned tonight what it's like to be human. You found out how to err. Now let's put you up, and we'll keep the whole episode quiet."

"Thanks, Taylor. I promise you that you won't regret it."

Chapter Fifteen – Liftoff

Houston, the fourth largest city in the U.S. with a population of more than four million, had as its namesake, General Sam Houston, leader of the Texian Army—the original army of Texas people—that won independence for the Republic of Texas. Despite its historic past, however, Houston was not regarded as a tourist destination. Unlike its counterparts, known for their financial markets, arts and entertainment, and scenic vistas, Houston prided itself as a city for doing business, from big oil, petrochemical, and energy corporations to individual entrepreneurs flaunting their success. Home to a world class Medical Center, renowned universities, and major sports teams, Houston—the first word spoken on the moon—was the epicenter of NASA's space program with its Johnson Space Center.

But today, as dawn broke on Saturday, the third of March, Houston would begin celebrating its Texas heritage with a parade through downtown with more than fifteen trail riding groups. Doctors, lawyers, rocket scientists, professors, CEOs, entrepreneurs, and citizens from one of the most diverse populations in the country on this day would line the streets to kick off Houston's biggest party—its annual rodeo. For two weeks, A-list celebrities would provide nightly entertainment to sold-out crowds and modern-day cowboys would compete in all the classic western events.

The smell of bacon cooking over the fire awakened Moira, torn between hunger pangs from a stomach still on Eastern Time and a reluctance to leave the warmth of her bedroll. She nudged her sleeping husband. "Time to roll, love," she said. "I'm hungry."

Crawford stirred, crawled out of his bedroll, and began dressing—cussing about his frosty clothes. Once dressed, he went outside to help one of his ranch hands finish preparing the breakfast.

"I won't be long," Moira said.

On his third cup of coffee, Crawford sat close to the fire and watched the first rays of the morning sun pierce the horizon. At sunrise, the bustle of activity from the other riders increased, with cooking pots clanking and conversations beginning.

When Moira climbed down from the wagon, Crawford fell in love with her all over again. She wore tight denim jeans with a dragonfly embroidered on each hip pocket, a leather vest over a white, long-sleeved shirt with a red kerchief around its collar. Her black Stetson hung at her back from a strap around her neck so that her hair, brown, tinged in locks of gold, framed her face. As she neared Crawford, he complimented her for her red boots and gave her a hug, unable to resist the temptation to pat both dragonflies. "Easy, love," she said, nodding toward Kazuhiro in his bedroll near the fire. "We're not alone."

Crawford prodded Kazuhiro with the toe of his boot. "Wake up, Rawhide," he said. "Big day ahead. Almost time to hit the trail."

Moira grinned at the sight. *If ever the people at NASA could see Kazuhiro, the physicist with a mind of unequaled brilliance, being treated like an everyday ranch hand, they'd never believe it*, she thought. *I love the way my husband and he get along together.*

Kazuhiro groaned, but stretched and began moving, shivering in the cold, morning air. When all were seated around the fire, the ranch hands served a country breakfast complete with biscuits and gravy, sausage and bacon, hash browns and scrambled eggs. Kazuhiro wolfed his down and asked for seconds. Moira smiled. *The man's got the metabolism of a gerbil*, she thought.

Before long, the bugle sounded the call to mount up, and Crawford suggested that Kazuhiro drive the cart and follow him and Moira on their horses. Kazuhiro gave him no argument about riding in the cart, happy to leave the horses to those more used to them. Crawford reviewed the parade lineup on the flier given him by one of the organizers. "We're right behind that group of barrel riders over there," he said, motioning to a dozen young women already mounted on their horses. Once the women took their place in line, Crawford led the Victoria Trail Riders and fell in behind them, Moira on his right, displaying the American Flag and Crawford displaying a Texas Flag. The parade began and worked its way through deep canyons—not of red stone but of glass-lined skyscrapers.

A few miles south of the parade at Ellington Field, Brady Olsen and Ashlyn Johnson, each wearing a helmet and flight suits, prepared to board their twin passenger jet for the trip to Cape Kennedy. Ashlyn hugged her sister, Jaelyn, and held her in an embrace longer than normal. "Bye, sis," she said. "You know we'll stay in touch—we always do."

Jaelyn didn't want to let her sister go, either. "Promise you'll stay safe?" she said.

"Promise."

The two broke apart and Brady and Ashlyn climbed into the cockpit of the craft and lowered the canopy. Brady started the engines and brought them up to speed while checking the controls. He signaled the lineman to pull the chocks. The two snapped a smart salute and Brady released the brakes and began taxiing the plane. Ashlyn gave her sister a crisp thumbs-up which Jaelyn returned, despite tears flowing down her cheek. Reaching the departure runway and gaining clearance, the plane lost no time accelerating for takeoff and in a graceful, climbing arc, turned eastward toward the Cape.

Two days later, the Eagle 2M rocket stood poised for launch at the Cape, bathed in brilliant lights in the pre-dawn darkness. Dressed in spaceflight gear and helmets and lying on their backs, Brady and Ashlyn waited through the final countdown stages. In a balcony overlooking Mission Control, Moira watched the calm activity of the technicians. Seated next to her were Taylor, Andrew, Jaelyn, and Kazuhiro. A row behind them and to their right were Jerome Mosby and several astronauts destined to fly future Ares missions. Each group talked among themselves but barely acknowledged the presence of the other.

Two hundred miles above them, Isaiah Wilson, Edward Matthew and Cosmonaut Vadim Azarov watched the horizon from the bridge as the ISS neared Florida. The docking crew was in place, ready to greet Brady and Ashlyn when they arrived and to help Eddie and Vadim board the Eagle 2M capsule for return to Earth. It relieved Isaiah to see Vadim leave the station because he was the cosmonaut who most worried Isaiah about his motives.

Halfway between Houston and Amarillo en route to his ranch, hauling a thirty-foot, gooseneck horse trailer filled with his two horses and his golf cart, Crawford pulled his diesel pickup into a truck stop. Inside the convenience store, he joined a crowd of people standing around a TV set, watching the launch preparations.

The final seconds of the countdown went without a hitch and Brady and Ashlyn felt a huge vibration and heard a deafening roar as the five Eagle 2M first stage engines ignited. Angry clouds of smoke and steam billowed from the launch pad and obscured the view of the rocket. Then the rocket rose from the pad and arced toward the heavens, trailing a brilliant cone of flame.

"Liftoff! We have liftoff of Eagle 2M taking two crew members on the first leg of their mission to Phobos," a public address announcer said, using a voice of high-fidelity tones.

Moira and the other people in the balcony stared at the huge video screen in the front corner of the control center, spellbound by the rocket's ascent, yet collectively holding their breath and praying for a safe flight.

Isaiah watched the brilliant point of light rise to the heavens and begin its journey to connect with the station. The next day, after closing on the station for several orbits, the two craft were in sight of each other, and Brady positioned the Eagle 2M capsule for the docking maneuver.

Ed and Vadim hurried toward a readiness room adjacent to the docking port to don their gear for the return trip home. Aided by technicians, they were soon suited up and ready, helmets at the standby. Isaiah joined them a few moments later.

Before long, people on the station could see the capsule approaching, enlarging in several minutes from a white speck in the distance to an object filling their whole field of view, thruster rockets firing in winks to adjust its trajectory for docking.

Brady guided the probe of the capsule into the drogue for capture and docked with a slight jolt. With a flurry of activity inside the station, techs secured the capsule to the port and equalized the pressure within the airlock. They opened the hatch, and assisted Brady in exiting the capsule, followed by Ashlyn.

Isaiah greeted the newcomers with a hearty welcome and introduced them to Eddie and Vadim. After a few additional pleasantries, technicians helped the two returning astronauts board the capsule and closed the hatch for the flight home. A slight shudder could be felt within the station as Eddie undocked the capsule and fired its thruster rockets to position it for the retro burn to begin their descent.

"Let's go to the bridge," Isaiah said. "We can watch the first leg of their return journey from there." He escorted Brady and Ashlyn through a system of passageways, sometimes walking horizontally and other times climbing vertical ladders. "You'll learn the route before too long," Isaiah said.

From the bridge, the three watched the capsule. When it reached the precise point for the reentry burn, it fired its retro rockets and began the fiery descent to Earth. The station traveled halfway around the Earth and was out of the line of sight, however, before the capsule's parachutes were deployed over the White Sands missile range, lowering it to a successful landing.

Techs and managers had reconvened at Mission Control and cheered at the sight of the landing, helicopters arriving to assist the astronaut and cosmonaut out of the capsule for the trip to Houston. Moira breathed a huge sigh of relief. She turned to look back over her shoulder at Jerome and acknowledged the success of the launch and safe return with a subtle nod of her head. *One launch down and one to go*, she thought. *Then we'll begin the voyage to Phobos.* Mosby gathered up his astronauts and left, not acknowledging Moira's gesture of goodwill.

Crawford remained inside the store. A man out of the crowd approached him and asked a question, not looking directly at his face. "Did you swap the device?"

Crawford answered, "Yes." He fumbled in his pocket a minute and retrieved the twenty-seven pin connector he had taken from Taylor's key chain. "Here's the old one," he said, and slapped the unit into the hand of the man. Without another word, Crawford left the store and returned to his truck.

A few days later, Andrew and Taylor walked the flight line at Ellington, preparing for their trip to the Kennedy Space Center. Jaelyn accompanied the two and stood beside them when they reached the NASA training jet. "This is the second time in a week that I've said good bye to someone close to me," she said. She hugged Taylor and gave him a lingering kiss.

"How about me?" Andrew asked. "I've never been kissed."

Taylor and Jaelyn both laughed. "Come here, Andrew," Jaelyn said. "I've never kissed an android, either."

Jaelyn embraced Andrew and to his surprise, planted a firm one on his mouth. "You keep my guy safe," she said. "I'm counting on you."

At a loss for words, Andrew remained silent but shook his head in the affirmative.

"Okay, you two, enough," Taylor said, stepping in between them. He whispered a farewell into Jaelyn's ear and hugged her again.

"Come back to me," she said, her voice husky with emotion.

Andrew climbed the ladder into the cockpit, again dressed in his polo shirt with the NASA logo and khaki trousers. He snickered at Taylor's clumsy ascent in his G-suit and helmet. "Fragile passenger coming aboard," he said. "Needs oxygen and can't take a few Gs."

"Okay, tin man," Taylor said. "Let's see if you can still fly this bird."

While Andrew brought the engines up to speed and signaled for the chocks to be removed, Taylor watched Jaelyn and gave her a final wave as the plane pulled away.

Taylor had flown with Andrew before, but each time he had to calm his nerves, knowing that he was riding in a complex, and potentially hazardous, machine being operated by another machine. But after takeoff it didn't take Taylor long to relax because Andrew flew the plane with a deftness envied by even the most experienced pilots, never deviating from the flight path nor being abrupt in using the controls. When they arrived at the Cape, Andrew flew the descent, keeping the glideslope instrument's crossbars centered on the correct path, as if they were painted on the gage.

Three days later, after a successful launch and a trip to the station in the Eagle 2M vehicle, the two joined their Ares crew members to begin the final preparations for their mission.

Chapter Sixteen – Launch

Thursday, March 15—the Ides of March—the entire NASA organization focused on its most momentous day since the initial launch of the Space Shuttle more than fifty years before. The balcony above the Mission Control Center overflowed with NASA executives, including Moira and her counterpart, Jerome Mosby, plus astronauts and mission specialists for future Ares missions. At NASA headquarters in D.C., Administrator Robert Durand and other top level managers were perched in a conference room watching a HD video feed from Mission Control.

Aboard the International Space Station, those not actively involved in the launch preparation process were viewing the action on video monitors positioned throughout the station. Isaiah Wilson, who would rather have been in the airlock with the crew members, occupied the bridge and followed the proceedings from a bank of screens.

At the hatch for the Ares I vehicle, the four crew members were having the final pre-flight checks performed on their space suits— all except Andrew, of course, who didn't need one. Now completed, the fueling process had taken eight hours, but the fuel umbilical remained attached to the tanks on the vehicle to replace even the slightest amount of fuel lost through venting so that the tanks would be full when the vehicle departed.

Under the watchful eye of Mission Control, the techs helped Ashlyn enter the command module first and secured her in her seat beside the H-B equipment. Taylor boarded next and settled into his seat next to Ashlyn. Pilot Brady Owen, a descendent of a long line of military aviators dating back to WWII, honored a superstition by removing a wad of gum from his mouth and slapping it on the side of the vehicle as he entered. Andrew followed Owen and occupied the commander's seat.

In a series of practiced moves, the techs closed the hatch and checked its security. One secretly removed the gum from the side of the vehicle, cautioning the others not to let anyone inside the vehicle know it had been done.

In the capsule, Andrew and Brady began a long list of pre-flight actions, confirming each step with Mission Control. Moira took a deep breath upon hearing Mission Control give the command, "Ares I, you're 'GO' for disconnect."

The video monitors showed the vehicle separate from the station and, propelled by small thrusters, shrink to a small, white dot—a point far enough away from the station where the main engines could be ignited without risking damage to the station.

Andrew precisely aligned the vehicle to the correct position and paused, awaiting the command from Control.

"Ares I, you're 'GO' for trans-Mars injection," a voice from Mission Control intoned without any hint of the enormous significance of the command. "On my mark, initiate a five-minute, thirty-seven second burn."

Several seconds later, "Mark!"

Andrew pressed the ignition button and said, "Here we go!" The four crew members were pressed into the back of their seats by the acceleration, their bodies shaking from the vibration. Andrew spoke to Brady in a voice loud enough for all to hear. "Once the burn is complete and the engines are shut down, Mission Control will verify we are established on the correct trajectory. Then in four days, we will reach a point where we can deploy the photon sail."

Brady had performed this sequence of actions dozens of times in the simulator with Andrew and knew full well the timeline without being reminded. Brady also knew the thrust created by the sail would be tiny compared to that of the rocket engines, but it would provide a constant acceleration for the duration of the flight, allowing the craft to reach an enormous velocity while conserving fuel for the return trip.

Right on schedule, the rocket engines shut down, having inserted the vehicle into the trans-Mars trajectory with none of the nightmarish emergencies that had been thrown at the crew during the simulator sessions.

NASA Administrator Durand, accompanied by FBI Agent Emmett Nelson, burst into Moira's office and wasted no time on civilities. "The FBI has informed me that there is a possibility that the android aboard Ares I has been injected with a virus."

In shocked disbelief, Moira looked at Agent Nelson and said, "That can't be."

Nelson explained that the FBI had intercepted communications about a "device" implanted in Andrew. "We're not certain about what kind of device it might be or how it may have been implanted, but the intercept is credible. We have to proceed on the assumption that it is factual."

"We can't abort the mission on an assumption," Durand said. "Is there a way to send a warning to the crew without the android hearing it?"

Her mind still reeling, Moira thought through some possibilities, at first drawing blanks. Then an idea came to her. "Yes, there is."

Moira explained that each day, at 8 a.m., Houston time, Taylor checked all of Andrew's systems.

"How does that help?" Durand asked.

"Taylor shuts Andrew down during the test—it avoids discomfort for Andrew. The test takes several minutes, and Andrew is unaware of anything during the check—like you and me being under a general anesthetic."

"Get a message put together and warn the crew tomorrow morning," Durand said. He stared at Agent Nelson. "What kind of a virus?"

Nelson explained that the simplest type might cause a complete destruction of the android's ability to think or move—like being in a coma.

"We could survive that," Moira said. "We have a multitude of backups in place for just such a possibility."

"That's why we think the virus would be more insidious," Nelson said. "One that would cause a subtle deterioration of the android's mental capabilities, unknown to the crew and even the android himself at the onset. He could progress toward dementia, or perhaps, even psychosis."

Face reddening, Durand challenged Moira in curt terms. "Get contingency plans together for the possibility of a goddamned demented, psychotic android." He spoke even harsher to Agent Nelson. "Call in every FBI resource available and root out the saboteurs—I won't refer to them as hackers—and hope to God we don't have a catastrophe before we find them."

Durand paused a moment to be certain his comments had made an impact and then turned to depart. "I'll call the Secretary of State and let him know we could be facing a major problem with the Russians, the Chinese, or some other country trying to sabotage our mission—or it might be a simple case of a twelve-year-old playing with his computer and creating havoc."

Durand stomped back to his office.

Moira asked her aide to schedule a meeting with her staff. "Top priority—ASAP!" she said.

She grabbed her coat, intending to take a walk in the courtyard to clear her mind, but encountered Jerome Mosby outside her door.

"I hear we've got a sick robot on board," he said, enjoying the accusation.

"Not exactly," Moira said. "There *is* a possibility our android has a virus, and for the sake of the mission, I hope our two organizations can work together to address the situation."

"Of course, but you're going to have to be ready to listen to reason."

"Just what does that mean?"

"We may have to put the robot . . . uh, the android to sleep— *for the sake of the mission.*"

"I am aware of that, but doing so will be a last resort."

"It may be the only resort."

The next morning a few minutes before 8:00, Taylor told Andrew to raise his shirt. "Okay, pal, you know the drill. I'm going to turn you off for a few minutes and check out all your systems. Don't get any thoughts about turning yourself back on. Remember, we removed that little shunt in Houston before we left."

Andrew complied with the request but was none too happy about doing so. Once Taylor switched Andrew off, he inserted the twenty-seven pin connector and began downloading the data.

A radio call came through to Brady from Mission Control. He was asked if the android had been shut down. When Brady confirmed he had been, Mission Control stated, "Senior Director Lambert has a message for the crew. We've set up a secure transmission for her. Here she is."

The sound of Moira's voice shocked Taylor, and it put him even more on edge when she singled him out. "Taylor, no one besides the Ares I crew and myself can hear this transmission," she said. "Until I am finished, do not awaken Andrew."

Moira conveyed the information about the possibility of a virus that might be more sinister than from a simple hacking. She described the potential hazards to be alert for and cautioned the crew to take decisive action in the event that Andrew showed any signs of instability. "We're on top of this and hope to be able to provide you more information in the near future. Until then, take extreme precautions. Do not leave Andrew unattended at the controls. It is my hope that this is a false alarm, but we cannot risk making that assumption."

Taylor struggled with his conscience. He had not told anyone about the shunt that Andrew fabricated and installed. But once it had been discovered and removed, Andrew's systems checked out perfectly, so Taylor had seen no need to pass the information on. Now Taylor worried that perhaps there had been some residual indicators from that installation that caused NASA to suspect a possible virus. *What if my failure to report the incident causes the mission to be scrubbed?*

Taylor looked at Brady, who with an almost imperceptible shake of his head, indicated that Taylor needed to keep quiet about Andrew turning himself on and showing up at the bar.

Brady mouthed the words, "Don't get us in trouble."

Taylor finished downloading the data. He plugged the connector into his computer and felt a sense of relief when the analysis showed no areas of concern. "Ms. Lambert, Andrew checks out fine this morning. I see no evidence of a virus, and I am certain our software would detect one if it existed."

"You keep checking him routinely. Remember, as much as I'd like to think our program would detect any malicious codes, the concern is that we could be under attack from the most capable electronics gurus in the world."

"Will do, Ms. Lambert."

"Godspeed to you and the crew. I'll hand you back to Mission Control, and you can awaken Andrew after I'm off. Don't tell him about anything that transpired in this conversation."

With a few audible clicks, Mission Control came back on the line. Taylor awakened Andrew, who noticed right away that the time that had elapsed while he was asleep was longer than normal. "Why so long?" he asked.

"Sorry, pal. I messed up the first readout. Had to run the analysis over again. But don't worry, you're fine—as always."

Four days later, with the Earth shrinking to the apparent size of a dime and the moon appearing as a white pinpoint orbiting it, the Ares I vehicle reached the position in its trajectory where the photon sail could be deployed to provide constant acceleration. The sail had been unfurled and tested several times at the station but never before when connected to Ares I vehicle under actual circumstances.

Andrew showed no nerves awaiting the command, and the other crew members positioned themselves to get a good view of the deployment out the capsule's cockpit front portals. Communications from Mission Control in preparation for the deployment sequence were clipped but did not show any sign of the tension that pervaded the room. Everyone knew all too well that the mission depended on a successful deployment.

Moira watched the proceedings from NASA headquarters, trying to put out of her mind numerous failure scenarios, from the sail fouling, or ripping to shreds, or its electronic grid not activating or shorting out—to many others.

"Ares I, you are 'GO' for sail deployment at your discretion," came the command from Mission Control.

Andrew checked the small section of the panel filled with switches and indicator lights regarding the sail's parameters. He glanced at Brady.

"Looks good," he said. "You agree?"

"Go for it, Andrew."

Andrew raised the protective cover over the deployment switch and without hesitation, activated it. "Control, sail deployment initiated."

"Roger that."

Ashlyn gasped in awe when she saw the cap on the bullet-nose protrusion on the front of the capsule blown away and the tightly packed sail ejected from its housing, trailing hundreds of strands of the high-tensile fiber that connected it to the capsule. A few minutes later, she felt a slight tremor when the sail bundle reached the end of its tethers.

When he saw a green light flashing beneath a second covered switch on the panel adjacent to the first one, Andrew raised the cover and activated the switch. "Control, sail being unfurled."

"Roger, Ares I, everything still 'GO' here."

In the distance, Ashlyn could see a ring of points of light, the circle growing larger as the miniature thruster rockets pulled the sail outward to form its one-mile-diameter canopy. Once the sail unfurled, the thrusters went out, and Ashlyn could see nothing but blackness. She began to worry.

"Shouldn't it be working by now?" she asked.

Brady turned to her and said, "A few minutes longer. It takes some time for the sail to fill with the photons emitted by the sun."

On the panel, Andrew could see the tension levels build in the tethers, confirming that the sail was beginning to provide an acceleration force.

Then, as if in a dream, the entire view in front of them became filled with the almost imaginary, multi-colored hues of an aurora borealis, in ever-changing patterns, swirling and dancing in a kaleidoscope of pastels.

"Oo-o-h! So beautiful," Ashlyn said. "I could watch this forever."

"Well, six months anyway," Andrew said. "Control, photon sail successfully deployed. We're on our way to Phobos!"

Chapter Seventeen – Mid-Course

More than three months en route, the activities aboard the Ares I vehicle had become routine—on the verge of boring, except for the exhilarating view out the cockpit ports. The spellbinding montage created by the flickering borealis never repeated its pattern, always providing new and spectacular combinations of shimmering hues. Earth had faded in size to a bright star, the moon no longer visible to the naked eye. Through the central aperture in the sail, Mars had become a red star, but neither satellite, Phobos nor Deimos, could yet be seen.

The crew had worked out sleep, exercise, bathroom, and eating schedules so that they didn't stumble over each other nor did they violate anyone's sense of privacy. Because of tempers being chafed by the compact and sterile environment within the capsule, there had been several arguments, sometimes followed by an extended period of no communications among the crew members.

At one time, Brady had become sickened by an intestinal virus, accompanied by vomiting and explosive diarrhea. The interior of the capsule smelled worse than the inside of a septic tank and cleanup in the near zero G environment was worse than disgusting.

During the times of duress, the crew took their emotions out on Mission Control, using language not suitable for public airwaves and calling individual controllers derogatory names. The crew had learned during their extended stay experiments at the Johnson Space Center that it was better to take out their grievances on the controllers rather than their other crew members or even worse, themselves. NASA had white-washed the depravities faced by the crew during testing, keeping under cover the real behavioral issues faced by the crew during an extended mission.

Unaffected by biological issues, Andrew remained at his station, taking only periodic breaks to flex all his joints to keep them from stiffening, much like his human counterparts. The other crew members kept a wary eye on his activities for any sign of confusion or malfunction. None had been observed, and the crew members had relaxed their vigilance to a degree, but not entirely.

At present, Brady and Taylor were in the crew quarters, Brady sleeping and Taylor relaxing by listening to music through his ear buds.

In the seat behind Andrew, Ashlyn wore the en route uniform, a navy polo shirt with the NASA logo, black shorts, and lightweight sneakers fitted with special soles for a better grip in the 1-G gravity of the vehicle. As she had done many times before, Ashlyn activated the H-B equipment and began responding to questions from Kazuhiro Sora, stationed outside an isolation chamber with Jaelyn inside. Ashlyn would think of an answer to Kazuhiro's question and radio it to Kazuhiro. Jaelyn would type the first answer that came to her mind for Kazuhiro to view on a monitor in front of him.

"Color?" he asked Ashlyn, a question that could also be heard by Jaelyn.

Blue, she thought for a minute before transmitting her answer to Kazuhiro.

Kazuhiro smiled and made a note when the word "Blue" appeared on his monitor, typed by Jaelyn. The twins had reached a ninety-five percent level of correct responses in their tests. Their success rate was more than triple the value that would have been attained by non-twin test subjects sitting adjacent to each other without the aid of the H-B field of particles to amplify their cognitive abilities. Yet the twins were more than twenty-million miles apart.

"Good work, you two," Kazuhiro said. "Now let's make it more difficult." He turned off the speaker in Jaelyn's chamber. "Only Ashlyn will hear the question—not Jaelyn. I will not know Ashlyn's response until after Jaelyn types her answer. That takes me out of the equation to make certain Jaelyn is truly reading Ashlyn's mind—not mine."

They had been at this testing for more than an hour, and inside the chamber, Jaelyn began to show weariness from mental fatigue. When words came to her mind, she typed them down: Black . . . Star . . . Ten . . . Square. Shaking her head in frustration, she struck out "Square" and replaced it with "Circle."

Struggling to find the next thought, she wished the test could be over. She closed her eyes and let her sub-conscious processes take over, undirected by her conscious mind in any way. Completely relaxed, she had the sensation of a hand on her knee, the pressure light at first, but increasing then becoming a caress, ending with a squeeze. Startled, she opened her eyes and realized in an instant what must be happening. She thought of the safe word she and Ashlyn had agreed to, concentrating on it as hard as possible. "Bail, Bail, Bail." At the same time she pressed a panic button that had been installed inside her chamber to alert Kazuhiro as to what was going on. As soon as he heard the alarm, Kazuhiro radioed Ashlyn with an alert.

Ashlyn awoke from a deep, subliminal state and realized that Andrew had his hand on her knee in a most personal manner. "Stop it!" she screamed, bolting upright and slapping the android's hand.

Her violent reaction shocked Andrew, and he jerked away his hand, making a feeble attempt to apologize for his forwardness. "Sorry," he said. "I don't know what came over me."

"Andrew, you can't do that," Ashlyn said. "It's socially unacceptable. I can't allow you to take that kind of liberty with me." She struggled to find the right words. *I told Jaelyn I could handle having Taylor making a move on me, but I never thought it'd be an android I'd have to worry about*, she thought. "Worse, it could mean you have a . . . uh—" she said, but not wanting to finish her thought and imply that Andrew might be dealing with a virus. *God, I hope that's not what's happening*, she thought.

"I had a human urge," Andrew said. "Ever since Jaelyn kissed me on the flight line, I've wondered about what it'd be like to approach a woman. I'm really sorry. You know I can't do anything more, don't you?"

"I know you're not capable of reproducing, and it must be very frustrating for you. You've never had the human experience of growing up and learning how to approach women—believe me, they're complex. Men have to find a way to make a woman interested in them, with a lot of subtleties and nuances required. Most times things don't work out. But, Andrew, you and I can only be crewmates and friends. Don't make me lose confidence in you by trying to make anything more of it than that. We've got a long way to go before we finish this mission."

"Okay, Ashlyn. I understand," Andrew said. "But it seems like I'm always coming up short on the human side."

"There isn't one of us that doesn't think of you as an equal. Why else would we ride with you on a mission like this? You have three human lives in your hands, and we trust you."

Taylor poked his head back into the cockpit. "Anything wrong?" he asked. "Did I hear someone yell?"

"Everything's okay, Taylor," Ashlyn said. "I banged my elbow on the H-B equipment getting out of my seat." *I'll fill him in later*, she thought, still worried about the reason for Andrew's indiscretion.

★ ★ ★

Watching the morning news, Moira sipped the last of her second cup of coffee, keeping an eye on the time she needed to begin the dash for the Metro Station for her daily commute to work. Paying idle attention to the morning anchor, she snapped to full alert when she heard breaking news about Russia calling for an emergency session of the U.N. Security Council and accusing the U.S. of violating the international treaty for peaceful use of space.

The bulletin outlined the Russian statement accusing the U.S. of destroying four of the five Russian probes to Phobos and calling for the U.S. to abort its Ares I mission and provide restitution to Russia in the amount of $176 billion for its losses.

No sooner had she heard the news than did her phone ring and the caller ID showed it to be NASA Administrator Durand. "Have you heard the news? Meet me at the State Department as soon as you can get there," he said. "Mosby's on his way. We've got one hell of a problem."

Moira stashed her cup in the sink and grabbed her coat. While taking the elevator down, she tabbed a text message to her staff. "Headed to State. Give me any pertinent information you have about the Russian accusations."

Reaching the street level and not having the luxury of waiting for the arrival of the next Metro train, she hailed a cab and jumped in. "State Department," she said. "Hurry!"

In the crew quarters during the next shift, while Andrew and Brady were at the controls, Ashlyn let Taylor know about the incident with the android and of her concern it might be due to the progression of a virus.

Taylor reassured her that Andrew's action was more likely due to his complex software trying to mimic human behavior than a virus. "He and I had a talk about it before we left," Taylor said. "I know the poor guy is bothered by his so-called 'urges.' He's resigned himself to wait until an upgrade is developed to allow him to fully function in that regard."

"So you're not worried?"

"Not at this time. Remember, I check him every day. Besides, don't you think that desiring someone as sexy as you is normal?"

Aggravation flared up inside Ashlyn. She bit her tongue and managed to tone down her reply. "Careful, Taylor. That's close to the line. You can't blame a victim for the aggression—women have been fighting that line of thinking forever. You just think I whacked Andrew. You keep on, and you'll see how hard I *can* punch!"

Taylor raised his hands, palms outward, in submission. "Whoa!" he said. "I meant nothing of the sort. I don't understand."

"That's exactly the problem," Ashlyn said. She exhaled and changed her line of thought. "I'm sorry. We've been a long time in cramped quarters, and we're all on edge about Andrew."

"I know. And . . . I'm sorry, too. But you and your sister are still pretty."

Ashlyn doubled up her fist and shook it at Taylor, but with a smile on her face.

★ ★ ★

When his aide opened the door for her, Moira dashed into the office of Secretary of State Cal Maxon. Administrator Durand and Jerome Mosby were already inside, along with the U.S. Ambassador to the U.N., Sharon Barstow. The secretary made all the introductions and said, "We have a few minutes before the Russian Ambassador, Vladimer Menik, arrives. He apparently wants to offer us—for lack of better words—an out-of-court settlement, so we don't have to drag this whole mess through the U.N."

"The Russian accusation is preposterous," Durand said. "We've had nothing to do with the loss of their probes."

"You and I both know that, but they believe they can make a case. We'll have to see what their facts are."

Maxon reminded everyone that the Russians had accused the U.S. of destroying their probes and was promptly interrupted by

Durand. "It's nothing but bullshit. They lost contact with their probes because of their own ineptitude. Nothing more sinister than that."

Maxon persisted. "They plan to go public at the U.N. and say we have discovered with our Martian landers that both Phobos and Deimos are artificial satellites placed there eons ago by extraterrestrials."

"Why in heaven's name would that cause us to destroy their probes?" Durand asked.

"The Russians believe we are covering up our discovery to avoid a world-wide panic. They feel we are taking drastic measures to prevent them from being able to expose our finding."

A knock at the door interrupted the conversation. "The Russian Ambassador is here, sir," said the aide.

"Send him in."

Everyone rose when the Ambassador entered, shook hands with him, and introduced themselves. Maxon offered Menik a seat and gestured for the others to sit, too. "Ambassador Menik, you requested an audience with us, so please tell us what you wish us to do."

The Russian looked around the room, gazing for a moment on each face, before he spoke.

"The prime minister has asked me to make an offer, which, if accepted, would allow us to withdraw our request for an emergency Security Council meeting." He withdrew a piece of paper from his attaché case. "I have it here if you wish to hear it."

Maxon saw that Durand was fuming, but his own tenure in the diplomatic corps allowed him to remain calm. "Go ahead, please."

The Ambassador read the offer verbatim. "Russia will withdraw its request to the U.N. if the United States will compensate Russia in the amount of $176 billion dollars for the loss of *Fobos 5*—using the Russian pronunciation—and—"

"Unacceptable," Maxon interrupted, waving his open palm at Durand to keep him seated.

The Ambassador glared at Maxon and continued. "—and agree to abort the Ares I mission."

"Not possible," Moira said, ignoring all protocol. Maxon raised his eyebrow at her indiscretion.

"Hear him out, Ms. Lambert," Maxon said.

"That's the prime minister's offer," Menik said. "Once accepted, the details can be worked out."

"Why the hell would we ever agree to something as ridiculous as that?" Durand said.

This time, Secretary Maxon stepped toward the Ambassador and apologized. "Forgive us, sir. My colleagues deal with rockets, not diplomacy." Maxon continued, his expression turning into a scowl. Standing within a few inches of the Russian Ambassador's face and using low, clipped tones unheard by the others, he said, "Now you tell me, sir: why the hell *would* we ever agree to something as ridiculous as that?"

Unflustered, the Ambassador answered the question. "Because we think you need our help."

"With what?"

"We understand the android aboard your vessel has been infected with a virus that will make him become unstable and dangerous. He could cost the lives of your crew."

The bastards, Moira thought, *they're the source of the virus.* On the verge of losing her temper, she kept quiet after Maxon waved her off, too.

"How could you help?" Maxon asked.

"We believe the software we've developed to ward off cyber attacks from you and other nations can neutralize the virus. If you agree to the offer and give us access to your android, we'll fix the problem."

Beside himself with anger, Maxon threw away any semblance of diplomacy and yelled, "That does it. Get out of my office and take your goddamned offer with you."

The Russian calmly placed the offer on Maxon's desk, closed his attaché case and stood. Before leaving he said. "I must inform you that you have seventy-two hours to accept our offer, or we go public with our demands."

Still holding himself in a posture of decorum, the Ambassador strode out of the office and closed the door behind him.

Her mind still whirling from the discussion with the Russian ambassador, Moira approached her office and saw FBI Agent Nelson seated in the foyer waiting for her. *My God, what else is in the mill today?* She wondered. He got to his feet and greeted her, asking if he might have a moment to talk with her.

"Of course," she said. "Come on in."

The agent pulled an iPad from his jacket pocket, tabbed the screen a few times, and began speaking, referring to his notes.

"We've had Astronaut Edward Matthew and Cosmonaut Vadim Azarov under surveillance ever since they returned to Earth from the station a few weeks ago," he said.

"And—?"

"We believe Matthew is clean, but it's a different story with Azarov." Agent Nelson explained that, acting on a tip from Chief Astronaut Isaiah Wilson, Azarov had been sending encrypted messages to a source inside the U.S., usually in Texas.

"We can't tell who the recipient is yet, because they use a prepaid phone—a different one each time—to communicate."

"What are the messages about?"

"We've not been able to decode much at this time, but we're getting close to breaking through the encryption—it's pretty damn sophisticated. One word keeps popping up, though—android."

Moira shook her head. "That could be entirely innocuous. Anyone talking about the mission would be likely to use that term."

"I agree, but the other word we've been able to decode is: virus."

Moira's stomach sent a pang through her mid-section. She caught her breath and asked the obvious. "Who do you think the recipient is?"

Agent Nelson snapped his iPad shut. "We don't know, but we have some suspicions."

"Who?"

Nelson stood and placed his iPad in his pocket. "Ms. Lambert, I'm sorry, but I'm not at liberty to discuss that information at this time. Once we have a better handle on it, I'll let you know." He turned to leave. "Thank you for your time."

Chapter Eighteen – Orbit

The angry, red surface of the planet Mars filled the aperture in the sail. The spacecraft had slowed to less than 5,000 mph as it closed in on Phobos—now visible as a grayish-brown, irregular shaped object, looking like a huge potato. Andrew and Brady were directing the vehicle in the initial stages of entering an orbit in tandem with the fast moving moon. Thirty-two hours away from reaching their desired position, the two worked through a pre-entry checklist, cross-checking speeds and coordinates provided by the onboard computer without the real-time ability to verify the data with Mission Control due to the forty-minute delay in communications.

Taylor, after finishing a twelve-hour shift in the cockpit, plopped into his bed in the crew quarters and fell sound asleep. Ashlyn, wanting to be at her very best when it came time to operate the H-B equipment, finished a sponge bath and began toweling herself dry. A surge of anxiety coursed through her body, not about the experiment, but about the forthcoming orbital maneuver. *This is where the Russians ran into trouble on several of their probes*, she thought. *What's out there waiting for us?*

The more she tried to put her apprehensions aside, the more prominent they became, torturing her mind with nightmarish images of the things that could go wrong. *We could enter too steep of a descent and crash into Mars. Or, if our descent were too shallow, we could career past Mars and continue into deep space*, she thought. In that case, they would perish in a prolonged death from asphyxiation when their oxygen ran out, but the craft would continue on, like an interstellar hearse, exiting the solar system with four dead bodies aboard. *Well . . . three at least,* she mused. *Andrew would last until his batteries were exhausted. Then he'd be lifeless, too.*

She wrapped the towel around her and struggled, hands trembling, to knot it. Then she thought about the whole business of alien ships attacking the Russian probe from the surface of Mars. *What if the extraterrestrial conspiracy rumors were true?* She shuddered at the thought. *We could be blown to pieces and never know what hit us. At least it'd be fast.*

In the cockpit, the atmosphere remained disciplined and all business. Andrew's hands flicked over the switches on the panel, activating vital systems at the precise time specified in the manual. Brady followed him through, checking off commands from his list as the items were completed, knowing that his duty represented a façade. *The damn bot never misses a trick,* he swore to himself. But then, after thinking it through, Brady knew he wouldn't want it any other way.

Taylor awoke to the sensation of a woman crawling into bed with him. He stirred, realizing that it was Ashlyn next to him under the covers without a stitch of clothing on. She pressed her entire body, already warm from her bath, against him in a steamy embrace. He opened his mouth in surprise, but Ashlyn placed her hand over it. "Sh-h-h," she whispered. "I want you to take my mind off my fears."

Moira's aide interrupted her work. "Agent Nelson is on the line. Shall I put him through? He says it's urgent."

"Yes."

After her aide closed the door, Moira grabbed the phone and answered.

"Ms. Lambert, this is Agent Nelson. I have some news for you that you need to hear before it hits the public airwaves."

Several thoughts coursed through her mind—all negative—and her heart beat peaked with trepidation. She didn't know whether there had been a catastrophe of some sort with the mission or worse, if Crawford had been injured or—God forbid—killed in an accident. But she never anticipated the scenario Agent Nelson outlined for her.

"Your husband has been arrested as part of an espionage sting and is being detained at a Federal facility in Amarillo."

"Arrested? You must be mistaken. On what charges?"

Agent Nelson explained that Crawford had been indicted as a key participant in an international ring that had the objective of sabotaging the Ares mission.

"That can't be," Moira said. "You don't have the whole picture."

"I'm afraid I do, Ms. Lambert. Your husband is scheduled to be arraigned in a Federal Court in Houston next Monday, along with two others. Our case is solid."

"Others? Who?"

"One is Cheng Hsu, a Russian agent who fronted as a representative for a fictitious Chinese wind turbine company. The other is Cosmonaut Vadim Azarov."

"I have to see my husband."

"Sorry, Ms. Lambert. He'll remain in our custody until the arraignment. Immediately after he's arraigned, a detention hearing will be held. If the judge determines he's not violent or a flight risk, he may allow him to post bail and be free on his own recognizance until the trial. You could see him then, but I must caution you, bail is rare in federal cases."

Moira mumbled a thank you and hung up. She gazed out her window, trying to clear her mind. After a few minutes, she buzzed her aide. "Clear my calendar for next week and book me on a NASA jet for a flight to Houston on Sunday. No other passengers besides me."

"Yes, Ms. Lambert. I'll get you the schedule when the flight's booked. Will you be needing a room?"

"I will."

Ashlyn moaned with pleasure. She had had lovers before, but they had taken a lengthy time to become familiar with the techniques that excited her and some men never learned them. Though this was her first time with Taylor, it was as if he knew what she desired even before she became conscious of it herself. Every caress, brush of his lips, flick of his tongue, touch of his hand or a trace of his fingertip aroused her desire. *Of course*, she thought, *he's learned the techniques from Jaelyn.* Ashlyn's breathing became rapid, each intake a gasp and then she arched her back as waves of ecstasy cascaded over her.

She clenched her arms around Taylor and pulled him to her. "Now!" she said. "Come to me, now." All her fears about the danger they now faced were driven to the far recesses of her mind by her desire. She let everything go, moving her entire body in ways to return to Taylor the pleasure he had given her. In moments, Taylor had to stifle a groan himself, as his passion reached its climax.

As he lay beside her, trying to catch his breath, Ashlyn whispered to him, "Jaelyn must never know about this. I love her too much, and this happened in a weak moment millions of miles away from home. We don't know if we'll ever get back or not, but if we do, she can never know about this. It will not happen again."

Taylor nodded his affirmation. "It's just a damn good thing that H-B equipment wasn't on for the last ten minutes. She would've known."

"Oh, shit. I forgot about that. We've got to fire it up in a few hours to scan the surface of Phobos."

"She'll be able to read your mind. You can't even think about this while it's on."

Ashlyn fought a sense of panic that welled up within her. A look of anguish crossed her face. Struggling to maintain her composure, she said, "The more I would try not to think about it, the more it would come to my mind. I can't erase the thought."

"Do you ever fantasize about things?"

"Of course I do."

"Well, then. If it ever comes up, you can tell your sister it was a fantasy. She'll understand. She probably has some of her own."

Ashlyn thought about that for a minute and then agreed. "You're right. I've even stumbled into one or two of Jaelyn's fantasies during our work. I didn't think anything of it, nor should she if the situation were ever reversed. Don't you think?"

Taylor took a long moment before answering. "I don't think it should ever be put to the test. We've created a real mess here. On one hand, you say this won't ever happen again, and I'm not too sure how I feel about that."

"And the other hand?"

"And the next time I'm with Jaelyn, will I be thinking about her—or *you*? And you, the next time you see your sister and me together, what will you be thinking? Maybe I should just back away from both of you."

Chapter Nineteen – Arraignment

Moira's cab lurched to a stop in front of the U.S. Federal Courthouse in Houston. She paid the fare, rushed through the security check at the entrance, and hurried into the courtroom through its massive double doors. She grabbed a seat in the visitor's section and caught her breath. A few minutes early, she tried to catch the eye of her husband's attorney, but he was preoccupied with a team of lawyers from his firm, seated behind the table for the defendant.

The bailiff at the door to the judge's quarters stood and spoke in a commanding tone, "All rise. The honorable U.S. District Court Judge, James S. Duncan, presiding."

Moira rose, as did all the others present, as the judge entered and took his seat.

"Be seated."

The judge reviewed the court document on his desk. "In the case of the United States versus Crawford R. Lambert, I instruct the bailiff to escort the defendant into the courtroom."

Moira's hands tensed around the arms of her chair, as she waited for her husband's entrance.

The bailiff opened the door and escorted Crawford, clad in an orange prison suit, to his seat.

Thank God he's not in shackles, Moira thought, but she was chagrined at the sight of him wearing cuffs. He glanced at her, and she raised her hand to shoulder height, giving him a wave with her fingertips. *He looks tired,* she thought. Responding to her subtle wave, she saw the flicker of a smile on Crawford's face before the bailiff turned him toward the judge. Crawford's attorney stepped to his side.

"Mr. Lambert, it is my duty to read the charges brought against you," Judge Duncan said. "Then I will ask you how you plead."

Crawford nodded.

"You are charged with: 1) conspiring to commit the criminal act of sabotage to undermine the ability of NASA, a government entity, to safely complete its Ares I mission to Phobos, and 2) espionage for attaining information for the purpose of undermining the government of the United States."

The judge removed his glasses and stared at Crawford. "Do you understand these charges?"

Crawford's attorney whispered an instruction.

"I do, Your Honor."

"How, then, do you plead?"

"Not guilty, Your Honor."

"Your plea is accepted. You are instructed to appear in this courtroom, at 9:00 a.m. on the seventh of May for your trial." The judge struck his gavel three times and then continued, "Now, without objection, we'll move into the detention hearing."

Moira listened intently to statements made by the prosecutor, recommending no bail be allowed and for Crawford to be detained in Federal prison until the trial. "The defendant is a flight risk," the prosecutor stated.

Crawford's attorney made the case for him to be released upon his own recognizance.

The judge called both attorneys to his bench and consulted with them at length. Asking them to return to their stations, he declared, "Bail set at $500,000. The defendant will surrender his passport to the court and remain in the United States until the trial is concluded." Again he banged his gavel and declared that the proceeding was over. The bailiff called, "All rise," and those present once again stood while the judge departed. The bailiff then escorted Crawford from the room.

Crawford's attorney packed up his sheaf of papers and stepped to the railing to greet Moira.

"We were fortunate. It is common in these cases for the defendant to remain in detention. The bail is pretty steep. Can you post bond?"

Moira nodded. "I'll not let my man spend another day in prison," she said, trembling with relief that her husband would soon be free, at least until the trial. She spent the better part of an hour with Crawford's attorney, working through the details of posting bail.

Once finished with the paperwork, Crawford's attorney said that it would take him the rest of the day to process her husband's release papers. "You should be able to pick him up before the court closes this evening."

Moira expressed her gratitude and left the building to find a place to have a bite of lunch. As soon as she stepped onto the sidewalk, she received a call from NASA Administrator Durand.

"Ms. Lambert, I must inform you that, until your husband is exonerated of all charges, I am placing you on leave from your duties at NASA. This is a mere formality because I hope to have your job status restored as soon as possible. Until this matter is cleared up, however, we cannot risk the perception of any conflict of interest."

Stunned by the message, Moira sat on the edge of one of the huge planter boxes on the plaza in front of the courthouse. "The timing could not be worse—right in the middle of our mission. I don't see how I can be replaced."

"I know that you and he are not on the best of terms, but I've asked Jerome Mosby to oversee your responsibilities in the interim. I'm sorry, Ms. Lambert . . . uh, Moira, I know how much you value your work and how good you are at it. I'd hoped you could have been my replacement some day, but now . . . uh, well now . . . that doesn't seem to be likely."

The sun rose over the Martian horizon and bathed the Ares I vehicle and the satellite Phobos in light, the tiny moon close enough that it filled the entire aperture at the center of the sail. Andrew and Brady were following commands from the computer, adjusting the capsule's velocity to enter an orbit in tandem with Phobos, less than a hundred miles distant.

"Hey, you two," Brady yelled to Taylor and Ashlyn. "It's show time! Get to your stations. Sail jettison and orbit acquisition in less than an hour."

Ashlyn took her seat in the cockpit, awed by their proximity to Phobos, and activated the H-B scanning equipment. She could see with her naked eye the gridlines in one area on the surface that some of the activists claimed represented artificial markings—or perhaps structures. She couldn't wait to zoom in on the area to scan its age compared to the surrounding terrain. The equipment hummed while it performed the scan.

The data would have to be encoded and transmitted to the lab at the space center for analysis before anything could be determined for sure. She felt frustration at being so close, yet so far, from an answer to the question about the origin of Phobos, pondered by scientists and activists alike. *Kazuhiro, work your magic on the data*, she thought. *Damn it! I wish I could be there to see the results at the same time you do.*

Taylor crawled in behind Andrew. "You doing okay, pal?"

Andrew nodded, too busy to speak.

Taylor looked through the portal to his left and marveled at the details he could see on the surface of Mars. He felt a spiritual connection to the image, and his emotions overwhelmed him. *Three more missions and man will land on that planet*, he thought. *Wish I could be one of them.*

"Pilot Brady, switch to communications channel 360.75 and put on your headphones for a classified and personal transmission," came the message from Mission Control.

Brady switched as directed and listened as Mission Control advised him of the developments at home, explaining the situation about Crawford's arraignment and his charges of participating in a conspiracy for the purpose of sabotage and espionage related to the Ares I mission.

Holy shit! Brady thought.

Mission Control continued. "We are now almost certain that Andrew has been infected with a virus that could jeopardize the safety of all aboard. And we must inform you that Senior Director Lambert has been placed on leave for obvious reasons. Your three passengers, Andrew, Taylor, and Ashlyn, are now under the command of your boss, Jerome Mosby until the issue is reconciled. We recommend that you not disclose this information to the others and that you remain especially vigilant. You may return now to the open communications channel."

Brady switched back to the normal channel.

"Anything wrong?" Taylor asked.

"No . . . uh, well yes," Brady said. "There's an illness in my family, but things should be okay."

"Sorry," Ashlyn said.

"Prepare for sail jettison in two minutes," Andrew said. "We'll fire the forward thrusters to slow our vehicle enough to stabilize our orbit as soon as the sail is released."

Ashlyn held her breath while awaiting the command. Taylor kept a close eye on Andrew.

"Jettison!" Andrew said, hitting the switch to activate the explosive links in the tethers to the sail. A staccato series of flashes lit up the view, indicating the tethers had been severed.

"Fire thrusters!" Andrew said. He opened the protective cover above the switch and pressed it.

The deceleration pressed the four of them against their restraining harnesses. They watched in awe as the sail began to diminish in size as it coasted away from the capsule, still exhibiting spectacular mosaics of swirling pastels from the photonic aurora.

"Stable orbit acquired," Andrew said, shutting down the thrusters.

Ashlyn let out her breath, relieved that the maneuver had gone so well.

A brilliant explosion of light filled the cockpit window, blinding the crew members, followed by the impact of a tremendous concussion against the capsule. The control panel lit up with annunciator lights and the sounds of multiple alarms filled the cockpit. Out of control, the spacecraft began tumbling, pitching, rolling, and yawing, worse than anything the simulator had been able to throw at them at the space center. Terror overcame Ashlyn, and she grabbed Taylor's arm and squeezed it to a point that he grimaced in pain.

"God help us," she prayed.

Once she got Crawford back to her hotel room, Moira embraced him with all the emotions of the day cascading over her. Never one to cry before, her sobs racked her shoulders.

Crawford tried to comfort her, but she wouldn't let go. "I couldn't bear seeing you go to prison," she said with her cheek pressed into his chest.

"I'm not going to go to prison," he said, stroking her hair.

She broke her embrace, throwing her head back to stare into his face. "You damn well could—and it might be for the rest of your life."

Crawford caressed her shoulders. "Let me worry about that."

Moira stiffened and said, "It affects both of us. With one phone call you could end all this, and you know it."

"Hon, this is bigger than both of us. I can't do that. There's more to be done."

Moira's emotion turned to anger. "Well, you might succeed in destroying both of us."

Puzzled, Crawford asked her to explain what she meant by that. She told him about the call from the NASA Administrator putting her on leave.

"—for perceptions," she said, her voice with an edge to it.

Crawford was at first shocked and then filled with remorse that his actions had caused her to lose her job. He walked her to the couch and sat her down next to him. He searched for words of consolation, but none came.

Before he could speak, her phone rang. Seeing the call was from the administrator, she answered it, trying to mask her feelings. "Hello."

"Ms. Lambert, you must get to the space center as soon as possible."

"But you put me on leave."

"Listen to me. Mission Control has lost contact with Ares I. Get over there now. Mosby needs all the help he can get."

She hung up the phone and grabbed Crawford's arm. "We have to get to the space center. There's an emergency."

They rushed to the street and hailed a cab.

Once at the center, Moira kept flashing her I.D. card, directing the cab to Mission Control.

Upon entering the building, Crawford was challenged by the guard. "I.D. please."

"He's with me," Moira said without pausing. She rushed down the corridor and after cautioning Crawford to remain in the hall, burst into a private room overlooking the control center. She interrupted Jerome Mosby briefing a group of managers. He waved her over when he saw her enter.

"We've got a real problem," he said. He explained in detail the situation, and it was no better than the administrator had described. "We've lost all contact."

"What happened?"

"We don't know. Everything was going extremely well until a few seconds after they jettisoned the sail. The cockpit camera transmitted a brilliant flash an instant before it went out. And their radio transmission ended with a high-frequency spike."

Jerome slumped his shoulders. "I must be honest. We can't be sure our spacecraft hasn't been destroyed—with all its crew."

Moira covered her mouth with her fingertips, her mind trying to absorb everything Mosby had said.

"Mission Control is trying to reestablish communications. If we can do anything to help them, we need to do it," Mosby said.

A thought occurred to Moira. "I'm going to the lab," she told Mosby. "I may be able to help. Keep me posted." Stepping outside, she grabbed Crawford's arm and pulled him behind her.

As they regained their vision, the crew members saw the sail no longer held its circular shape, but was ragged instead. An entire sector had been shredded and was dark. At the boundary of the darkness, an electrical arcing, like that of an intense lightning storm, expanded and swept across the remaining portion, until the whole sail had been destroyed.

"Mission Control," Andrew shouted. "We're in trouble." He realized his mic was dead.

For the first time ever, Andrew, even with his superb, robotic algorithms, could not control the wild, vertigo-inducing oscillations of the capsule. He yelled at Brady to join him on the controls. "Take the yaw axis," he said. "I've got pitch and roll."

Brady joined Andrew in the fight to stabilize the capsule, handling the joystick with years of fighter plane experience. In time, the oscillations slowed but could not be completely controlled.

"I've got it by myself now," Andrew said. "Assess damage."

Both pilots inventoried the panel alarms and annunciator lights. The report was dismal.

"Our high-gain antenna is out of commission. We've lost all communications with Control. We also lost our fix on the sun and that's why the gyros tumbled," Brady said. "You'll have to control the ship manually until we can reset them."

"Anything else?" Andrew asked, remaining calm.

"Cockpit pressurization is okay. Crew environmental and oxygen systems are functioning properly, but we've lost half of our solar panels. Available power is down to forty percent."

"Cut any unnecessary uses of power," Andrew said. "We lose that and we're done."

Ashlyn shut down the H-B equipment. Taylor fought his way into the crew quarters and turned off all lighting and heating systems.

Brady worked feverishly to reset the tumbled gyros by providing a manual fix on the sun. In several minutes, the gyros spooled up again and to everyone's relief the capsule stabilized.

When the capsule's motion settled down, Brady looked toward Andrew and said, "What the hell happened?"

As calm as ever, Andrew said, "We were hit by a beam from Phobos."

"What?"

"I think when we jettisoned our sail, somebody—or something—interpreted it as an aggressive action."

"If that's the case, we're a damned sitting duck."

"You're right. I think the sail took the brunt of the beam. We got hit by a deflection. We won't be so lucky the next time."

Chapter Twenty – Peril

Moira rushed into the simulator lab, dragging Crawford behind her and answering every security challenge to his presence by flashing her badge and offering the terse comment, "He's my responsibility." When the security guards saw "NASA Senior Director" on her badge, they backed down and allowed their passage. It was out of character for Moira to pull rank, but *this is a matter of life or death*, she thought.

She found Kazuhiro Sora in the electronics room, poring over analytical data from the scan Ashlyn had transmitted minutes before. As Moira entered the room, his eyes opened wide, and he frantically tabbed back and forth between the last few displays on his computer monitor. Startled by her entrance, Kazuhiro jumped to his feet, bowed and started to speak. "It's not—"

Moira cut him off. "You haven't heard?" she asked. "We've got an emergency."

She explained that they had lost all contact with the Ares I vehicle and the electronic signals at the time of the loss were indicative of an external event, perhaps even an attack of some sort. She stressed the point that they were unsure as to whether or not the capsule survived—or, worse—they could not verify the safety of the crew.

"We need your help," Moira said. "We've got to re-establish communications. Where's Jaelyn?"

The color drained from Kazuhiro's face. "I just talked to Ashlyn," he said. "And now you're telling me she might be gone?"

"We pray that's not the case, but that's why we need you and Jaelyn. Tell me where she is."

Kazuhiro scratched his head. "Ah, when we finished receiving Ashlyn's transmission, she left to grab a bite. Said she was going to the cafeteria."

"Call her and get her over here. Now!"

Flustered by the situation and by Moira's assertiveness, Kazuhiro fumbled with his phone and after a few miscues, managed to reach Jaelyn and get her on her way.

"Get your H-B equipment in the simulator fired up and ready for when she gets here," Moira said. "We've got to try and reach her sister."

"The H-B module in the simulator is just a basic prototype for local use. We've never tried to communicate with the Ares I capsule millions of miles away."

Aboard the capsule, the crew were taking stock of their situation and trying to save themselves. According to protocols worked out prior to the mission, Pilot Brady Owen could choose to assume command in case of an emergency. "Mission Control, I am declaring an emergency," he shouted into his mic, hoping that his transmission could be heard. He looked at Andrew. "Did you hear me?" he asked. Andrew nodded. Brady continued, "I am assuming command."

Brady held his breath a few seconds, worried that the android might resist. But Andrew obeyed the protocol without a hint of disagreement. "You've got the ship," Andrew said.

"All right, crew, let's go by the book," Brady said, trying to pull up the emergency procedures on the computer. The screen remained black. Nothing.

Going by memory, Brady tried several backup systems, but none worked. "They all rely on the same high-gain antenna that's been damaged."

"What about the antenna on the surface probe in the cargo bay?" Taylor asked.

"It wouldn't help. Only useful for a very short range, from the surface to the capsule."

"Can we repair the high-gain antenna by doing a space walk?" Taylor asked.

"We have some replacement sections in the bay, but from what I can see from here, most of our antenna is gone. Given enough time for several EVAs, we might be able to rebuild it enough to generate a weak signal, but even that is doubtful."

"We don't have that much time," Andrew said. "Using my memory banks, I've analyzed the electronic profile of the flash of light that hit us." As the rest of the crew listened, Andrew explained that the pulse of energy that hit the capsule had the characteristic signature of a laser. "It took an enormous amount of power to generate that beam. The only source of power on Phobos would be solar panels because as far as we know, there are no power generation plants."

"What does that have to do with the amount of time we have remaining?" Brady asked.

"Solar power couldn't provide enough energy by itself. The panels would have to feed banks of capacitors over a long enough time to build up sufficient voltage to create a massive, but short duration beam."

Brady began to understand the situation. "We have some time—but we don't know how much—before the apparatus can recharge and fire again."

"That's the situation."

"Well then, it's time for us to get the hell out of here."

Andrew shook his head. "Can't. We need the burn data and timing for the retro thrusters in order to initiate the slingshot maneuver, but our computer is down. We can't upload the information from Mission Control either. Not without our antenna. If we guess and we're wrong, we either crash into Mars or head off into deep space."

"Damn it! How long do you think we've got before . . . uh, whatever it was that fired at us goes for a kill shot?"

"I can make nothing more than an educated guess. We're a great distance from the sun. It'll take a long time to recharge the capacitors. So, maybe . . . uh, maybe as little as half an orbit around Mars while Phobos is in the sun. Once we go into the shadow again, I think we'll be safe."

"But we're not in the shadow yet—not for another three hours or so."

"I warned you. It's an educated guess. Until we get back into darkness, we risk being hit again at any time."

Listening to the conversation between the two pilots, Ashlyn felt icy fingers grasp her stomach. *My nightmare might be coming true*, she thought.

Jaelyn came into the room, out of breath from racing from the cafeteria. Moira briefed her on the situation while Kazuhiro booted up the H-B equipment. He tweaked the controls until he was satisfied with its operation. Crawford retreated to a seat in the far corner of the room, trying to stay out of the way.

Moira took him a set of NASA coveralls and handed them to him. "Crawford, if anyone comes in this room, you grab a broom and start sweeping. It's bad enough that I'm working when I'm supposed to be on leave, but if they ever find out that I've let an indicted saboteur in this classified area, I'll never get my job back and worse, they'll shackle you, put you in an ill-fitting orange jumpsuit, and throw you in federal prison with guys who would slit your throat for a single cigarette."

Moira left Crawford and joined Kazuhiro and Jaelyn inside the simulator.

"Ms. Lambert," Kazuhiro said. "What should we try?"

"We have to reach Ashlyn. Do whatever you think is necessary."

Kazuhiro escorted Jaelyn to the seat by the H-B equipment and placed a helmet over her head connected to the equipment with an umbilical cord. "In our later versions, we were able to develop a wireless connection," Kazuhiro said. He pulled an opaque visor down from the helmet's face shield, obscuring Jaelyn's vision of her surroundings. "Jaelyn, close your eyes and use the bionic relaxation techniques we've taught you."

Kazuhiro watched the gages that showed Jaelyn's blood pressure, temperature, and her heart and respiration rates. He studied his watch and whispered to Moira. "It's taking longer than normal. Probably due to her concern about her sister."

After several moments, Jaelyn's vitals reached a suppressed state. Kazuhiro spoke to her using a velvety voice. "Jaelyn, think about your sister. Stay relaxed and think only about her name, nothing more. Keep your mind open for her response."

Fifteen minutes passed and then thirty. No connection could be made. Kazuhiro did his best to keep Jaelyn calm, but with every passing minute, hope faded that her sister was still alive.

Moira saw teardrops trickle down Jaelyn's cheek and gave a worried glance to Kazuhiro. He shook his head and placed his index finger on his lips telling Moira to remain quiet.

Brady turned in his seat to face the other crew members. "I don't need to tell you. We're up shit creek. Any minute now we could get hit again. I'm going to try and back us away from Phobos using our thruster rockets. Maybe I can get us out of range."

"That won't work," Andrew said. "We can't waste the thruster fuel if we ever hope to align ourselves for the slingshot maneuver; we'll need them to dock with the station."

"We've got to do something."

Andrew turned around and stared at Taylor with an expression of sadness on his face.

"There's another way," Andrew said.

Taylor gave him a quizzical look.

"We've got a probe in the cargo bay that we planned to send to the surface of Phobos. It's sized to carry equipment to the surface on later missions, but it's empty for this one. I could ride it to the surface."

"What good would that do?"

"I know the coordinates of the laser. I could knock it out with nothing more sophisticated than a sledge hammer. Then you'd have time to rebuild the high-gain antenna."

"But you'd never get back to the capsule, pal," Taylor said.

Andrew hung his head. "No."

Taylor put his hand on his friend's shoulder. "We can't ask you to do that."

"You don't have any other choice," Andrew said. "Besides, it's what humans do for each other, isn't it? They fall on grenades. They take bullets. They make sacrifices."

Ashlyn hugged Andrew, tears in her eyes. "Are you sure?" she asked.

"I am. I'm not being all that noble. I must remember that I am merely a machine, a pretty complex one, but still a machine."

No one said a thing until Brady broke the silence. "All right, let's do it. Taylor, you help Andrew get through the airlock into the cargo bay. Don't waste any time. I feel like we're in the cross hairs of a huge cannon."

A security guard entered the simulator room. Crawford grabbed a broom and began sweeping, his back turned toward the guard. "What's going on in here?" the guard asked.

Crawford continued sweeping. "I don't know," he said. "They asked me to clean up this mess. They don't let me in on any of the technical stuff."

The guard peered through one of the portals in the simulator. He recognized Kazuhiro, but not either of the women. "That old physicist is pretty sly, sneaking in here to impress a couple of good looking broads. Hell, I'd take either one of them, wouldn't you?"

Crawford mumbled an answer the guard could not hear.

The guard glanced back and forth between the simulator and Crawford a few times and left.

Crawford let out a huge sigh of relief. Inside the simulator, however, the mood remained tense. Jaelyn had detected no response from her sister and a sickening fear overcame her that she might never hear from Ashlyn again. She ripped off her helmet in anguish and screamed, "It's no use. I can't keep doing this."

Moira grabbed her shoulders and shook her. "Put it back on," she said. "If you ever hope to see your sister again, you've got to keep trying. You may be her only hope."

Her cheeks wet with tears, Jaelyn looked into the eyes of Moira, like a child being chastised by her mom. "Okay," she said, putting her helmet back on. "I'll keep trying."

Inside the airlock, Taylor helped Andrew gather up a few needed items, putting off saying farewell to his friend as long as possible. When he could stall no longer, Taylor spoke a few words of advice.

"Remember, Andrew, the Phobos gravity is so slight you'll almost be weightless. The probe is designed to grip the surface, but anytime you are outside, make sure to be tethered. We don't want you flying off into space, pal."

Andrew nodded.

"And once you finish disabling the laser, get back into the probe and stay there. It'll give you some protection against solar rays and micro-meteorites."

"Why should I be concerned about that?"

"You want to preserve yourself for rescue."

"Rescue?" Andy said, "Why would NASA risk trying to do that when they could just build another machine like me—even better this time? You're talking about rescue just to make me feel better."

"Stop it, pal, we can't give up hope." Taylor swallowed, experiencing difficulty with talking about Andrew's next move. "Andy, the only way for you to survive a year or more is to put yourself into hibernation."

"You mean turn myself off, don't you?"

Taylor hesitated before answering. "Yes."

"And before we started this mission, we removed the little shunt that let me turn myself back on, didn't we?"

"You know we did."

"You are telling me that I'm going to die, aren't you?"

"Look, pal, you are not going to die. I promise you that on the next mission we'll boot you back up."

"But, even if you can convince NASA to rescue me, it's going to be at least a year. Maybe more."

"It'll be the blink of an eye to you."

Andrew whispered a line from a long-forgotten poem about how one should approach death, "—like one who wraps the drapery of his couch about him and lies down to pleasant dreams."

"You're not going to have to worry about that," Taylor said.

"Prove it to me, Taylor."

Taylor thought a long time before answering. "Do you remember talking about humans making sacrifices for each other?"

Andrew nodded.

"Well, humans do something else for each other and sometimes it's even more difficult than making sacrifices."

A look of bewilderment crossed Andrew's face. "What?"

"They trust each other. You must trust me, pal, to do what I say I am going to do."

Andrew stared at Taylor, trying to comprehend. "Trust? I'm not sure I'm programmed for that."

"You are, but it's down deep inside you. Reach for it."

"I'll try. But right now I'll have to take your word for it."

"That's what trust is all about, pal."

A green light above the cargo bay indicated it was time for Andrew to enter.

"Before you go through the hatch, here's something to take with you in case you need them," Taylor said. He handed Andrew a small metal box.

"What's in there?"

"Fused explosive bolts. We had some spares with us in case the ones installed failed to work. They'll be more effective than a sledge hammer on the laser device—we don't have a sledge hammer on board, anyway. And you might need them for something else."

"What?"

"In case you run into aliens," Taylor said, trying to lighten the mood. "Of course, they may be more scared of you than you would be of them."

"Thanks, Taylor—for everything." Andrew said. He depressured the airlock and turned toward the exterior door. "But promise me something else."

"Anything."

"When they get that new model of android perfected—the one that's fully capable of sex—order me an upgrade and have it ready when I get back. It'll give me something to look forward to!"

They both laughed. Taylor stepped out of the air lock and secured the inner door. He watched Andrew open the outer door and step through it into the cargo bay. Before closing the door, Andrew turned back toward Taylor with a smile on his face and gave him a farewell wave.

Chapter Twenty-One – Contact

Andrew stabbed a series of buttons to bring the probe's electronics to life. "Com check," he said.

"Loud and clear," Brady replied.

Andrew activated the turntable holding the probe. It began a one rpm spin to provide some gyro-stability to the probe. Satisfied that all was well, Andrew spoke to Brady through the mic, "Ready for launch."

Brady opened the clamshell doors on the cargo bay, and reflected sunlight from Phobos filled the interior of the cargo bay. "Launch at your discretion," he said.

Andrew activated the launch switch. The clasps holding the probe to the cradle opened and a coiled spring gently launched the probe. Once free of the capsule, Andrew watched the clamshell doors close behind him. He acquired a radar lock on the coordinates for the laser device and engaged the thruster controls. The probe drifted away from the capsule and accelerated toward Phobos. The probe's computer estimated touchdown in seventeen minutes, and once on the surface, Andrew planned to waste no time in reaching and destroying the laser facility.

The remaining crew members watched in fascination as the probe rapidly diminished in size until it became a mere point of light above the surface of the tiny moon.

An idea struck Ashlyn. She uncovered the panel on the H-B equipment and began to make a brief recording of the probe's landing, taking pains to keep the unit's power consumption to a minimum. "We'll have a record of what transpires," she said. "Kazuhiro can analyze the shape and origins of the laser device once we get back. If it's alien, we'll know for sure."

"What else could it be?" Taylor asked.

His question stumped Ashlyn. "I can't think of any other possibility," she said.

Ashlyn. Come on, Ashlyn, you've got to hear me. It's Jaelyn.

"Oh God, Taylor," Ashlyn said. "I just heard my sister."

"What?"

"It must have been because I switched on the H-B equipment, but I'm sure I heard her."

"Turn it off," Jaelyn screamed. "I can't take this anymore. This is more terrible than a séance—trying to reach a soul that's crossed over."

Kazuhiro reached to shut down the H-B equipment, but Moira prevented him from doing it.

"Not yet," she said. "Let her get hold of herself. We can't stop now." Moira put her arm around Jaelyn. "I believe your sister is alive," she said. "You must not give up. She's alive and you are the only one who can keep her alive."

The expression on Jaelyn's face suddenly changed from grief to that of elation.

Jaelyn, it's me, Ashlyn. I heard you!

Chapter Twenty-Two – Counterattack

Moira barged into a small conference room adjacent to Mission Control, interrupting a gathering of high-level NASA engineers huddled around Jerome Mosby. Mosby looked up with an expression of aggravation on his face.

"We've made contact," Moira said. "The capsule is safe."

"I have no idea what you are talking about," Mosby said. "We're hailing the capsule on every frequency possible and monitoring all the channels for a response. We've heard absolutely nothing since we lost all communications with them. I don't have time for this because I'm due for a press conference in twenty minutes."

Moira knew Mosby wouldn't be easy to convince. "We know they are safe."

"How?"

"From communications using the Higgs-Boson equipment."

Mosby tossed his tablet onto the table and stood fully upright. "Ms. Lambert, are we talking about ESP?"

"Not the proper term, but yes. The twins are in communication with one another."

"Can you provide me any substantiation of the status of the capsule that's not based on wishful thinking by some twenty-something girl about her sister?"

Anger boiled up inside Moira, but she kept it under control. "No."

Mosby grabbed his tablet and turned back to his discussion with the engineers, ignoring Moira.

"They need our help," Moira said. "They're in desperate trouble."

Mosby sighed aloud and excused himself from those around the table. "Okay, Ms. Lambert. You give me one solid piece of evidence, and I'll listen. Otherwise, you need to understand, I'm busy."

Moira searched her mind, frantically trying to think of something that would satisfy Mosby. Nothing came to her at first. Then—

"Ask me something about the capsule that only Brady would know."

"Ms. Lambert, this isn't some parlor game."

"Damn you. Ask me."

Mosby shrugged his shoulders, and pinched the sides of his nose with his fingertips, absorbed in thought. Then he tabbed a few commands into his tablet and brought up Brady's profile. "Give me his fighter pilot nickname—and his son's birthday."

Moira grabbed her cell phone and called Kazuhiro. She relayed the questions to him and told him to have Jaelyn ask her sister to get the answers. "Hurry," she said. "But the lives of the crew members depend upon getting the correct answer."

Kazuhiro didn't question Moira's intent. He told her to stand by a moment. The line remained quiet for what seemed forever and Moira worried that Kazuhiro may have lost the connection. She was about ready to redial when she heard his voice. She pressed the speaker button on her phone for all to hear. "Jaelyn says the answers are: 'Intimidator' and 'January 18, 2005.' For added verification, Brady offered his social security number if you want it."

"Go ahead."

Kazuhiro read the number, digit by digit, and repeated it to be certain Moira heard it correctly.

Everyone in the room kept quiet as they watched Mosby scan Brady's profile on his tablet. His expression changed from skepticism to amazement. "All three are correct!"

"Do you believe me, now?"

"I have no other choice. Tell me all you know about the situation."

Moira explained in detail about the spacecraft being targeted by a powerful burst of light, destroying its high-gain antenna. She told them that Andrew had launched the probe to Phobos, intending to destroy the laser facility. But before she finished, Kazuhiro jumped in. "Ms. Lambert, there's something else. I was about to tell you when you first showed up in my office. I got so busy trying to contact the capsule that I didn't have a chance to tell you before."

"Tell me what?"

"The Higgs-Boson analysis confirmed that Phobos is a natural satellite—not extraterrestrial. The geological anomalies on its surface have been there since the satellite came into being."

"Then who built the laser facility that fired upon our capsule?"

"I can't answer that. It's evidently too small a facility for the scanner to pick up."

Brady monitored the com channel from the probe as Andrew maneuvered for a landing.

"Touchdown," Andrew said, beginning the process of shutting down and stabilizing the probe. Once completed, he peered through the probe's single portal, looking for the laser facility.

"Got it!" he said, "It's much smaller than I expected, but I'm within a hundred feet of it."

"Tell him to be careful," Taylor said.

Andrew eased open the hatch of the probe, and before stepping to the surface of Phobos, he fastened his tether line to one of the brackets on the landing struts. Securing the other end to his belt, Andrew threw the loops over his shoulder. He grabbed the box of explosive bolts Taylor had given him, and a pry bar stored inside the door for use in case for some reason the hatch were to jam. *Old fashioned, but reliable,* he thought.

Hanging on to the rail on the steps with his free hand, he began his descent. The first step he took catapulted himself into an awkward somersault, his legs and arms flailing to regain his balance. He spun in mid-air until the tether stopped his drift with a jerk. It took more than a minute for the light gravity of Phobos to bring him back to the surface. He lay on the ground motionless until he figured out how to roll over and right himself without taking another vault into the atmosphere.

He found that if he remained on his knees, he could shuffle along with care and remain on the surface. The distance to the laser equipment now seemed much greater than it had before, and it took him twenty minutes before he reached it.

"I'm at the facility," he said, speaking into his mic. "You're not going to believe what I see."

"Tell us," Brady said.

"There're Russian letters and numbers all over the pieces."

Brady looked at the other two crew members. Neither had any answers.

"Can you take pictures?" Brady asked.

Andrew eased his tablet from his pocket and snapped a dozen photos, taking a selfie of him in front of the facility for good measure. *It'll give them a basis to measure its size,* he thought. He connected the tablet to his mic and transmitted the image.

"Holy crap!" Brady said. "That's what took a potshot at us."

"Uh-oh," Andrew said. "The barrel has started moving. Looks like the facility has re-activated and is sighting in on you for another shot."

"TAKE IT OUT!" Brady screamed.

Realizing he didn't have enough time to set the fused bolts and wait for them to blow, Andrew grabbed a bracket on the facility and began striking his pry bar at what appeared to him to be the most fragile parts of the facility's aiming mechanism. With no atmosphere to transmit sound, he could not hear his blows, only feeling strange vibrations through the hand which grasped the facility and the hand holding the pry bar.

Hitting harder and ever harder on a cover over the drive mechanism, Andrew finally broke it loose, leaving the gears and electronic controllers exposed. He smashed the controllers with all his strength. A shower of sparks erupted, and the gears stopped moving an instant before a blinding flash of a laser beam lit up the sky.

Inside the capsule, Brady flinched at the sight of the beam passing within a few feet of the spacecraft. "Jesus, that was close," he yelled. "Kill it, Andrew. We can't take a chance on another shot from it."

Andrew placed four of the explosive bolts on the mechanism and set the timers to a minimum, allowing him almost no time to retreat to safety. Once set, Andrew jumped into the sky, playing out the tether line as he rose. Reaching the end of the tether, he was again jerked. Tumbling like a rag doll, he rebounded toward the probe.

A series of four flashes along with puffs of white smoke tore the facility into shreds, a couple of pieces of shrapnel narrowly missing Andrew who was still struggling to regain control of his body's motions.

"We saw that," Brady said. "Did you get it?"

"Hang on!" Andrew shouted, careening toward the probe. He reached out his arms and legs just before he hit with a huge impact. The slack tether line wrapped around the probe's structure and prevented Andrew from bouncing back into space. Finally his oscillations ceased and Andrew stared at the remains of the facility. "It's destroyed," he said. "I'll send you a picture. You can call this one 'after.'"

Taylor grabbed the mic from Brady. "You all right, pal?"

"Other than my left arm being a little bent, I'm fine, but things got a little wild."

"We all send you our gratitude. You saved our lives. Thanks, pal."

"You're welcome, Taylor. Just remember your promise."

"I'll come back for you personally, and I'll have the new parts you wanted ready for you when we get you back home."

Chapter Twenty-Three – Slingshot

Satisfied that the laser complex had been destroyed, Brady hurried to make preparations to break away from Phobos. *Might be another facility*, he thought. *Can't take that chance by sticking around.*

Again he tried to boot up the computer and obtain the retro-rocket burn parameters, but the screen remained blank. Brady banged the keypad with his knuckles, venting his frustration.

"Taylor, see if Ashlyn can get the firing data from Jaelyn—she'll need to relay the numbers from Mission Control."

Jaelyn, sitting next to the H-B equipment in the simulator, sensed her sister's thought, *Need burn parameters.* But before Jaelyn could contact Mission Control for the data, an image flowed through her mind that shook her to her very core—Taylor and Ashlyn in bed together. The imaged devastated her, destroying her concentration. Sick at her stomach, she forgot all about the burn parameters. *Damn you, Ashlyn—how could you? You told me you could rebuff any of Taylor's advances, but you were the one that initiated the tryst.*

Jaelyn received no response from Ashlyn, as if the connection had been completely broken. She wasn't certain she cared or not.

Moira saw the expression of chagrin on Jaelyn's face and knew her session with Ashlyn had come to an end but didn't know why. Seeking to clear her own mind, Moira stepped through the hatch on the simulator and approached Crawford, still clad in janitor's clothing. "They're alive," she said. "They were attacked but now they are in a stable orbit in tandem with Phobos. Right now that's all we know."

"What's wrong, then?" Crawford asked.

"Something's happened between the two twins. They're no longer able to communicate."

"Give it time, sweetheart. Maybe they can work it out."

"I'm not sure."

Brady scowled at Ashlyn. Notepad in hand, he asked, "Have you got the burn parameters?"

Ashlyn shook her head. "I can't get them."

"What the hell is going on? I don't want to wait around for the possibility of some laser facility in another location taking another shot at us."

Ashlyn stared at Taylor and whispered, "Jaelyn knows about us. I couldn't keep it from her. I haven't been able to reach her since."

Taylor knew the two women might not be able to reestablish a connection for some time—maybe never. "Brady," he said. "We're going to have to try and repair our antenna. I think that's the only hope we have of reestablishing communications with Mission Control."

Brady tossed his notepad onto Andrew's vacant seat. He thought through the options for making repairs. It would go quicker if both Taylor and Ashlyn worked together on the EVAs, but he couldn't risk Ashlyn being away from the H-B equipment in case the connection could be reestablished. Neither could Brady himself go because if something happened to him, no one would be left to fly the ship. It had to be Taylor acting on his own.

"Get suited up," he told Taylor. "You're going outside to make the repairs."

Taylor retreated to the crew quarters and began donning his space suit. All the crew members had simulated the antenna repairs underwater at the Johnson Space Center, but it had always proven extremely difficult even with two people working together. He knew the odds for one person being successful were not good, but they had no other choice.

Once his suit had been pressured up and satisfactorily tested, Taylor stepped into the airlock. Ashlyn secured the door behind him and began the depressurization process. A green light by the latch on the door into the cargo bay indicated it was safe to open. Taylor took one last look at Ashlyn and gave her a thumbs up which she returned with a wave.

Taylor opened the door and stepped into the bay, struggling with his umbilical cord. He unlatched the cabinet on the side wall of the bay that contained the spare antenna elements. He removed the first element, nearly eleven feet in length and checked to be certain the tool he needed to fasten it in place was secured to the element.

"Open the hatch," he said into his mic.

The clamshell hatch began opening, a slit at first, but slowly expanding to fully open, exposing Phobos and the surface of Mars against the vast blanket of space. Because of the space craft's slow rotation, the planet, satellite, and the starry background gave the illusion of motion. Taylor had to concentrate on the fact that he was the one moving—not the heavens—to avoid motion sickness. He crossed himself and said a silent prayer. One arm holding the element and the other a vertical pole, he worked his way upward to the exterior surface of the capsule. Then, using handholds along the surface, he approached the antenna.

Seeing the damaged antenna close up, Taylor stared in disbelief at the amount of destruction. Fortunately, the base of the antenna where the elements were attached appeared to be okay. Locking his feet into the nearest handhold, Taylor used the tool to remove the element with the most damage. Once free, he shoved the old element into space, taking care not to let any of the sharp edges rip his suit, and watched it in fascination as it spun away, much like a tumbling, giant, black feather. He struggled to position the replacement element in place and then bolted it to the base, pausing frequently to flex his hand, cramping from the effort. When he finished, he grabbed the element and shook it to verify it was secure.

"One down," he said, out of breath. "Three to go."

"Copy that," Brady said. "Good work."

"Looks to me like if I replace the worst elements, we'll have about sixty percent of our original antenna available for use."

"We'll have a chance," Brady said. "Keep going, but don't get careless."

Taylor worked for two hours replacing the other elements. Exhausted, he climbed into the cargo bay for the last time, secured the tool back in the cabinet. He reentered the air lock, latching the exterior door behind him.

Ashlyn re-pressured the chamber and greeted Taylor when he entered the crew quarters, giving him an awkward hug because of his bulky space suit.

"Thank God, you're back," she said.

She helped him remove his helmet and climb out of his suit. Exhausted, he sat in one of the chairs in the crew quarters.

"Tell Brady to try the radio," he said. "I can't guarantee that I did any good."

★ ★ ★

The alarm sounded in Chief Astronaut Isaiah Wilson's chambers, alerting him to an emergency need for his presence in the central control room. Clad only in his coveralls, he scrambled through the door and saw his deputy at the console wearing headphones and beckoning for Isaiah to join him at the panel.

"I think we've got a signal from the capsule," the deputy said, "but I can't lock it in."

Isaiah grabbed a second pair of headphones and listened as the deputy tried to capture the signal. Then, Isaiah heard it, too. Filled with static and of varying strength, he could pull only a word or two out of the background noise. He scribbled them down as best he could.

The deputy kept fiddling with the electronics and finally captured the signal, very weak but readable. The deputy turned toward Isaiah. "They are asking for the retro-rocket burn parameters for the slingshot maneuver. Mission Control can't pick up their signal due to atmospheric interference. We'll have to act as the intermediary."

Isaiah contacted Mission Control. "We've got the Ares I capsule," he said. "They need the burn data. Get it quick before we lose their signal."

The deputy tapped Isaiah on the shoulder and pointed to some notes he had made.

"Control, the capsule mass configuration for the maneuver is its gross weight less the weight of the probe and four antenna elements—and the android."

"The *android*? Why is he not aboard?" Control asked.

"We'll let you know just as soon as we receive the burn data and transmit it to Ares I."

"Stand by. You'll get it within ten minutes."

Taylor copied the data relayed by the station and went over his notes twice to verify he had it down correctly. Once satisfied that he did, he handed the information to Brady.

"Computer's still fried," Brady said. "Get in Andrew's seat and follow me through. I'll have to do a manual burn."

After a tense countdown, Brady fired the retro rockets, and the capsule began its parabolic arc around Mars. From an orbit of 3,700 miles above the Martian surface, the capsule would descend to a point only fifty miles above the planet at its closest—no room for error.

Ashlyn gazed at the Martian landscape passing beneath her, fascinated by the details she could now see. As they neared the surface, Mars filled the entire sky, and the increase in velocity gave the illusion that they were skimming over an angry red mirage. The illusion was short lived, because they crossed into the dark side of the planet and were immersed in complete blackness. With the sun obscured, they had no visual reference as to their altitude.

Taylor prayed the parameters were correct and that they were not going to crash into the void beneath them. Unconsciously, he lifted his feet off the floor, as if he might prevent the capsule from sinking lower. He felt Ashlyn's hand on his shoulder, placed there for his reassurance. Fending off his own anxiety, he patted her hand.

Two hours passed and then the brilliance of the sun reappeared, dazzling them with its brightness.

"Three minutes until main engines start," Brady said, his fingertips raising the switch guard and hovering above the start button.

"Burn for eleven minutes and forty-two seconds," Taylor read from his notes. Aware that the engines had been dormant in deep space for more than six months, he closed his eyes and prayed. *Please let them all start and do their job without exploding.*

"Roger," Brady said, checking the setting for the burn duration.

The digital countdown timer for the burn initiation clicked to zero.

"Mark!" Brady said as he jabbed the button to fire the engines.

The whole capsule resonated with the roar of the main engines, and the crew members were violently jammed back into their cushioned seats by the force of the rockets. The main engines burn consumed the bulk of the reservoir of fuel in the tanks, lightening the vehicle's weight by half and leaving only a small residual for any mid-course corrections. The burn seemed to last for an eternity.

"Coming up on main engines shut down," Brady said.

Taylor nodded in affirmation.

"Mark!" Brady said, flipping the switch to shut down the engines.

The shut down of the main engines threw the crew members forward against their seat and shoulder restraints, and the sudden silence reverberated in their tortured ears. In the blackness of space to the left of the sun, they could see a tiny pinpoint of light.

"Earth!" Brady said. "We're headed home!"

Back at the space center, Moira rushed into the gallery above Mission Control, out of breath and dragging Kazuhiro—and Crawford—behind her. "Stay quiet," she told him. Joy filled her heart as she watched the excitement in the room below, shards of confetti cascading into the air.

Thank God, they're on their way home, she thought.

Chapter Twenty-Four – Justice

Moira watched from the visitor's section of the Federal court room as the trial proceedings for Crawford opened. Surrounded by a team of high-profile attorneys, Crawford wore a pinstriped business suit. His Stetson was absent, but his western boots were visible, extending beyond the legs of his trousers.

Crawford had not discussed any of the details of the case with Moira except trying in vain to reassure her that things would work out.

"Is the defense ready to make an opening statement?" the judge asked.

"The defense requests an extension," Crawford's lead attorney answered.

"On what grounds?"

"May we approach the bench, Your Honor?"

After the judge waved them forward, both the prosecutor and Crawford's attorney approached the judge.

Following a lengthy whispered, but animated, consultation, the prosecution and the defense attorneys returned to their separate tables.

"Extension granted," the judge said, striking his gavel. "This court will reconvene in one month."

The bailiff asked all present to rise, and the judge left the courtroom.

As soon as Moira and Crawford got into their car, she asked, "What was that all about?"

Crawford reached for his Stetson resting on the back seat and placed it on his head. A broad grin broke out on his face. "We need more time to be prepared."

Moira returned to her office in D.C., her leave of absence having been canceled by Administrator Durand on the basis that her leadership contribution to the safety of the Ares I craft far outweighed any negative perception brought about by her husband's legal issues. "We need you," Durand said. "Russia still plans to drag us through the U.N. limelight."

Trying to catch up on the events that had transpired on that issue during her absence, Moira was interrupted by a secure transmission from Isaiah Wilson.

"Ms. Lambert, I have some information for you."

"Nothing's happened to the capsule, has it?" she asked, holding her breath in anxiety.

"No. Everything's fine with them. They are about half-way home, and the mid-course correction went well. They are on track to arrive on schedule."

"Thank God," Moira said.

"But I need to pass along something else."

Moira listened while Isaiah explained that the astronaut who had replaced the Russian cosmonaut, found a thumb drive left in his quarters that contained a list of his contacts.

"The FBI will be interested in one of the names," Isaiah said. "Have your agent contact me, and I'll transmit the data to him."

"You can just send it to me, and I can forward it."

An extended pause.

"Ms. Lambert, I don't think that would be wise. Let's do it the way I suggested."

Moira agreed, but with a nagging concern about the person's identity in question.

Isaiah continued. "Now here's the clincher—something else I've chosen to withhold from Mission Control and give only to you."

"Go on."

"Despite the unusual circumstances, the probe—as designed—scooped a sample from the soil on the surface of Phobos. We just received the analysis."

In all the excitement, Moira had forgotten the original purpose of the probe. It was to determine the composition of the soil so that its ability to support a large landing craft carrying humans and cargo could be determined. Shaking her head, she told Isaiah she didn't have time to discuss that rather mundane data at the present.

"Ms. Lambert, I believe you need to know. It has a direct bearing on the whole situation."

"Okay, but be quick."

She listened intently as Isaiah told her the composition and nearly fell out of her chair when he said it. She asked him to repeat it to be certain she had heard him correctly. She ended the conversation asking Isaiah to tell no one—absolutely *no one*—about the information he had given her. Hanging up the phone with trembling hands, she thought through all the ramifications and began to piece together the motives of those who were attempting to sabotage the U.S. mission to Phobos.

Two weeks later at the request of NASA Administrator Durand, Moira and Jerome Mosby attended a top-level meeting with Secretary of State Cal Maxon and the Russian Ambassador,

Vladimer Menik to discuss the case Russia intended to bring before the U.N.

"We applaud you on the success of the Ares I mission and join you in wishing for a safe conclusion of that effort," Menik said. "Now that you have had that success, it is imperative that you agree to discontinue the remainder of your program—for the safety of your own astronauts. Otherwise, we will pursue a U.N. resolution to stop you."

"Ambassador Menik, I know of no reason for us to respond to such an outrageous demand," the secretary said.

"Russia claims Phobos as our sovereign territory, and according to international law your missions represent an encroachment of our boundaries."

"Claims?" Administrator Durand said. "What basis do you have for such a statement?"

"On our previous *Fobos 4* mission, we landed a probe on the surface of Phobos, and planted our flag on our new territory. Phobos is Russian sovereign territory."

The secretary scoffed at the ambassador's answer. "You know that according to international treaties, you have no more claim to Phobos than we do to the moon. And we planted our flag with humans—not some damned mechanical probe."

The ambassador assured Secretary Maxon that the treaties regarding territorial possession had been modified since the moon landings and that Russia would protect its territorial claim for Phobos through the U.N. where "the arrogance of the United States would be tempered by the court of global law."

Moira couldn't sit still any longer. She opened her briefcase and withdrew several photos, pictures taken by Andrew of the laser facility before he set the explosive charges with close ups on the markings.

"This picture shows a manufacturing nameplate—Manufactured in Vladivostok, 2028. And this one shows another nameplate—all in Russian script—clearly giving us proof of Russian responsibility for the facility."

Ambassador Menik looked through the photos and tossed them aside. "Fakes," he said. "Taken at your Phobos landing mockup at the Johnson Space Center. If you have nothing else, I'll be taking my leave."

"There's more," Moira said, handing the Ambassador a detailed report. "These are the results of our probe's sample of the surface soil on Phobos."

For the first time, a look of concern crossed Ambassador Menik's face. As he studied the data, Moira summarize it for him and the others present. "Platinum, more than ninety-nine percent pure. It is the most valuable, precious metal on Earth, rarer than gold and found only in diminishing quantities in South Africa. Once used for jewelry and catalytic converters, Platinum is in heavy demand for high-tech electronics and cyber weapons applications. Platinum from Phobos would provide the Russians a source of enormous wealth and a means to manipulate the worldwide supply of the metal—akin to oil for OPEC."

Moira paused a moment before continuing. "Platinum also accounts for the metallic signature and orbital dynamics that reinforced the speculation that Phobos was extraterrestrial. We now know that Phobos is *not* extraterrestrial but is instead a captured asteroid worth a fortune beyond comprehension."

"Perhaps," Ambassador Menik said. "But that has nothing to do with Russia."

"It has everything to do with Russia," Moira said. "Your *Fobos* probes were not lost at all. Each one succeeded. After your first probe found Phobos to be covered with platinum, the others were used to set up your defenses until you could make a manned landing and claim the moon as a Russian territory. The loss of your probes represented an elaborate fabrication for the purpose of covering up your discovery. You constructed a scenario of an extraterrestrial habitation of Phobos, hostile to any encroachment, to keep other nations away. When our Ares I mission was close to succeeding and threatened to blow your cover, you authorized a laser strike of our vehicle planning to blame it again on hostile extraterrestrials. Well, it almost worked, except that our vehicle survived the attack and discovered the truth."

"Truth?" Ambassador Menik scoffed. "Preposterous. It's nothing but absolute conjecture. You have no proof except for your fabricated photos and laboratory analysis."

"Mr. Ambassador, may you and your countrymen rot in hell for what you tried to do," Secretary Maxon said. "We will meet you in the U.N. or even on the surface of Phobos to see that right prevails. I don't think you want any of this to become public. By the way, your puny little 'defensive facility' has been destroyed. We plan to not only continue, but to *accelerate* our Martian exploration using Phobos as a base."

The ambassador remained stoic as he gathered his papers and stuffed them in his brief. "I shall relay your unfortunate comments to the prime minister. Good day, gentlemen—and Ms. Lambert. I'm sure we will see each other at a U.N. Security Council meeting in a few weeks."

The ambassador turned to leave but was cut short by Secretary Maxon. "One moment, Ambassador Menik, there's no way you or your country are going to pursue this with the U.N."

Menik chortled and again turned for the door.

Secretary Maxon buzzed his aide. "Send them in," he said.

Moira was surprised to see Agent Nelson enter accompanied by a Federal Marshal, but she was stunned when her husband followed them both into the room. The three men stopped inside the office doorway, positioned between the ambassador and the exit.

"Agent Nelson, I believe you have something to tell the ambassador," Secretary Maxon said.

"Ambassador Menik, you are being charged with espionage and with an attempt to sabotage our Ares I mission. Because of your diplomatic immunity, you cannot be arrested but you will be escorted to a flight at Andrews Air Force base that will take you directly to Moscow. You will be denied reentry to the U.S."

"Impossible. On what grounds?" Ambassador Menik. "I demand you put me through to the prime minister."

"In due time, but I have another duty to perform first." Agent Nelson faced Jerome Mosby. "Senior Director Mosby, you are being charged with abetting a foreign agent in the crime of espionage and you are under arrest." Agent Nelson withdrew a card from his vest pocket and read Mosby his rights. Upon completion, he nodded to the Federal Marshal. "He's yours."

When the marshal began cuffing Mosby, the ambassador stormed toward the door, but was halted by Agent Nelson. "You can't do this. You have nothing on me," the ambassador said.

"Let me introduce Crawford Lambert who will explain the situation to all of you," Secretary Maxon said. "Crawford is an undercover CIA agent who has been assigned to this case for several years. He has chosen to come out in order to help NASA and the United States eliminate this threat."

Crawford stepped to the center of the room. He presented the secretary with a box of thumb drives, cell phones, documents, videos, and detailed logs of his contacts and conversations the past few years. "All copies," Crawford said. "But here's the proof you need. When the FBI processes my information, they'll see that everything Senior Director Lambert has said is the God's truth. It will implicate Ambassador Menik as the leader of the effort along with many others who are complicit in the operation, including Cheng Hsu who worked for a wind turbine company that was a complete sham."

"What role did Senior Director Mosby play in this?" the secretary asked.

Crawford stared at Jerome. "He had no connection to the Russian leadership. No knowledge of their intent. However, we traced the source of the virus he attempted to introduce in Andrew back to him and two other members of his organization, one being Cosmonaut Azarov."

Secretary Maxon glared at Mosby. "Why?" he asked.

Mosby remained silent.

"Mosby tried to plant the virus not to destroy the expedition, but to make Andrew appear to be losing his mental capabilities. Not enough to cause a problem, but worrisome enough for Brady to have to assume command."

"But why?" the secretary asked again.

"Mosby wanted NASA Administrator Durand's job when he retired. He knew he faced stiff competition from Senior Director Lambert, and he wanted the failure of one of her developments, Andrew, to reflect poorly on her competence."

"But your android never showed any symptoms of the virus. Why not?"

Crawford explained that a Russian operative gave him a twenty-seven pin thumb drive he was to swap with the real one that Taylor carried on his key chain. In Houston, before he made the swap, he dropped the infected drive off at a CIA lab using the front name "Global Technologies."

"They scanned it and—using the most sophisticated electronics in our arsenal—found the virus, a nasty, spider-like series of codes with the bite of a cobra. One that, once injected, would replicate itself thousands of times and attack the android's higher level brain functions like cognitive ability, judgment, and logic."

"But it didn't work."

"It would have," Crawford said. "But the lab extracted it. The virus is so pervasive that the lab has it isolated in an electronic vacuum to take no chance of it escaping and infecting our own systems. When I swapped Taylor's thumb drive, I put the one on his key chain that had been sterilized. So Andrew was never at risk."

"How did Mosby obtain the infected drive?"

"Cosmonaut Azarov. The FBI arrested him in Houston this morning."

Now it was the NASA Administrator's turn to shake his head. "Once Ms. Lambert was placed on leave, Mosby had the inside track. It's ironic that some of the very difficulties he created allowed Ms. Lambert to demonstrate her abilities. She erased any doubt that she was the best choice."

Secretary Maxon turned to Agent Nelson. "Please take a couple of your agents and escort the Ambassador to the Andrews Air Base. Because of his diplomatic immunity, we can't prosecute him, but we have a plane waiting to take him to Moscow. I fear that he will face a far worse fate from his own government than we could ever provide. His failure will cause a consternation among the Russians that will never be erased. God help you, Ambassador, for Russia won't."

Everyone cleared the room except for the secretary, Crawford, and Moira. Crawford wrapped his arms around her and felt her tremble on the brink of sobbing. "Hon, now that I no longer have a job, I'm going back to the ranch," he said. "Want to join me there soon?"

Moira backed away from his embrace, looked deep into his eyes, and nodded.

Chapter Twenty-Five – Return to Earth

The brilliant, blue and white marble disk of Earth had grown to a size that it filled the portals on the capsule. Mission Control directed Brady through the process of a final burn to place the capsule in the same orbit as the International Space Station, now appearing as a bright star above the Earth's horizon. In two days, the station grew large enough to make out its shape, and twenty-four hours later, the docking maneuver was successfully completed. After a series of integrity checks, the occupants heard a banging on the hatch and Brady gave a thumbs up. The techs from the station opened the hatch and helped the three out of the capsule, giving them a round of high fives as they exited. Standing in the air lock was Chief Astronaut, Isaiah Wilson, a huge smile on his face. "Welcome home," he said as he greeted each of them.

A few days later, a crowd had gathered on the tarmac at Ellington Field in Houston to welcome the astronauts and specialists back home. Microphones adorned the podium, arranged like a nest of baby birds, beaks open, waiting for food. Reporters and TV cameras were in a roped area to one side. Administrator Durand stood with Moira, Crawford, and Kazuhiro at the front of the crowd, but Jerome Mosby was absent. Mission controllers, technicians, and any NASA members who played a role in the mission were present, eager to celebrate the success of the expedition.

The NASA jet pulled to the apron and its engines were shut down. An attendant opened the door and unfolded the stairs. The astronaut and mission specialists clad in NASA's navy blue jump suits—Brady and Taylor clean shaven and Ashlyn with her glistening blond hair bound in a pony tail—stepped down to the concrete to a round of cheers and applause. The three joined hands with Ashlyn in the middle and raised their arms victoriously with wide grins on their faces. A moment later Chief Astronaut Isaiah Wilson descended the stairs and joined them, happy to be a part of the celebration.

The administrator spoke a few words of welcome and congratulations and stood alongside them for official photographs. Once the strobe-like flashes from the cameras diminished, the three disappeared into the crowd to shake hands and renew friendships.

Kazuhiro buttonholed Ashlyn, thanking her for her contribution, but she seemed to be distracted, scanning the crowd for someone. Kazuhiro gave her a questioning glance.

"My sister. Have you seen her?" she asked.

Kazuhiro nodded to his left just as Taylor reached him. Ashlyn spotted Jaelyn about the same instant as did Taylor. He was stunned to see her in the arms of another man, an astronaut he knew.

Ashlyn approached her sister, desperately seeking some sign of forgiveness. There was none. Ashlyn reached out to hug her sister, but Jaelyn did not return it. Instead she introduced the man standing with her. "This is Jonathon Masters. Taylor, I'm sure you know him."

Taylor cleared his throat and shook Jonathon's hand. After a few awkward attempts at conversation, Ashlyn and Taylor left the two of them and entered the reception area, sat at one of the tables and ordered a drink.

"I guess we deserved that," Taylor said.

Stony silence.

"On the way home you talked to me about the possibility of leaving NASA," Taylor said. "Have you thought anymore about that?"

"I have, but I plan to stay."

"That'll be difficult."

"Easier than leaving. A friend told me one time that when you leave a bad situation, the shadows follow you," she said. "If I stay, Jaelyn and I can work through it, but it may take years. If I were to leave, I'd lose my sister forever and have to live with the shadows of her memory and of the way I hurt her."

Back outside, Moira grabbed Isaiah's arm and expressed her gratitude for his help. While she was speaking to him, Crawford talked to Kazuhiro about trail rides. "If you want, next year I could get you a spot in the rodeo as a broncobuster," he said with a grin, elbowing Kazuhiro in the side.

But Kazuhiro turned the tables on him. "I'll pass," he said. "But we need a custodian to sweep the floors in the lab. You demonstrated quite a knack for it. Interested?"

Both men laughed, and they worked their way through the crowd to the reception area.

The conversation between Isaiah and Moira turned to a serious note.

"Ms. Lambert, I understand you were offered the NASA Administrator's job."

"I was, but I declined."

"As far as I'm concerned, there could be no finer person to take that job than you. I wish you would have accepted the position. After all, we have seven more missions to complete in the Ares program."

"I know. And I feel the same way about you in your position. You are a fine man. As for me, it's time I do something I've longed for all my life."

Isaiah smiled. He had heard of her plans. "You're going to join your husband on the ranch in Amarillo," he said. "I wish you the very best."

Chapter Twenty-Six – Home

More than a year later, the sun neared the horizon, bathing the Caprock formations in a beautiful orange glow beneath a turquoise sky. Two riders in western gear picked their way along the trail to the top of the formation and neared Crawford's favorite old windmill, now in silhouette against the sunset. When they reached the windmill, they dismounted and stood arm in arm watching the western sky. A few moments after the sun slipped below the horizon, Moira spotted it first.

"Look!" she said, pointing to a brilliant star traveling rapidly eastward, "It's the station."

They remained silent for a minute. "Isaiah's back on board," Moira said, waving as if he might see her.

As they watched the station transit the sky, Moira said, "Ares II landed on Phobos this afternoon. What a perfect confluence of events."

Crawford drew Moira close to him and gave her a big squeeze. "Hon, you need to tell me something I've wondered about for a long time."

She turned to him. "What is it?"

"Well, you remember when I was in jail, you told me I could get released with a single phone call."

"Of course I remember."

"How did you know? How were you so sure I wasn't really involved in the plot?"

Moira laughed and placed her hands on his chest. "Easy. I've always known that you were in the CIA—even though we could never talk about it."

"But I still could have been a bad guy on the take."

"You could have, but I knew better. When you told me you were meeting with a representative from a wind turbine company and, for all the possible reasons, that you were considering entering into a contract to build a wind farm, right here, on top of your beloved Caprock, I knew it was a subterfuge. There's no way you would do that."

Crawford knew she was right. "The damn things are unsightly, noisy, and I don't think they are all that effective—even with the huge subsidies they are given."

Moira laughed. "Now you see how I knew you weren't involved. It's time for us to go back to the ranch."

The Ares II probe touched down on Phobos. An hour later a space-suited figure, tethered to the probe, descended the stairs to the surface carrying a United States flag. Once on the ground, the man planted the flag by twisting the auger on the staff deep into the surface.

He then turned toward the old Ares I probe nearby and shuffled toward it, fighting to maintain his balance in the low gravity. Nearing the probe, he glanced at the gritty dust on his white boots and pant legs, mentally calculating the value of the material on them. *Millions*, he thought. *Too bad the suit and the dust are NASA's property, not mine.*

He reached the probe and opened the hatch to look at the seemingly lifeless android inside. Opening a panel on the droid's chest, he inserted the twenty-seven pin probe and flipped a switch, praying sufficient battery power remained. He watched for a moment awaiting some sign of motion.

Andrew flicked his eyelids open, instantly recognizing Taylor's smile behind his face shield.

"Hey, pal," Taylor said. "I promised you I'd come back. Come on, let's go home."

Made in the USA
San Bernardino, CA
09 April 2017